FINDING

Ms. Wrong

LOVE SAVES • BOOK ONE

SUSAN WARNER

Finding Ms. Wrong
Love Saves

First Edition. June 8, 2020

Published by EG Publishing

ISBN: 978-1-948377-74-4

FINDING
Ms. Wrong

CHAPTER ONE

New York City
July

Smack, smack, smack.

The two sizes too small hot-pink flip flops snapped against Liam Butler's heels as he hurried down the alleyway. He tightened the towel, which barely covered his thighs, around him and let out a sigh of relief. He'd managed to escape his date by slipping through the bathroom window and had made it down the three blocks to his hotel.

As he headed for the building's rear door, he grimaced at the stench in the alley. When the slight July breeze came through, it brought a very pungent smell along with it.

The narrow passage was dark and he could hear some questionable movement in the back. When Liam looked on the ground, he had to avoid the murky puddles of what, he didn't even want to guess. "Ugh! I don't know what's worse, my situation or the smell of the garbage."

"Well, if you don't like the smell, you can leave," sneered

a voice. Liam turned to find who had spoken, but all he saw were some broken down boxes in the corner, a large dumpster, and some black bags.

"Come out! I'm Liam Butler. I own this hotel and this alleyway."

First, he saw a metal shopping cart filled with bags and a small dog on top. The dog was some kind of terrier, and at one time, it might have been white, but now was a dingy gray. The terrier eyed Liam as if he were a new toy. As the shopping cart came out from behind the dumpster, Liam saw an elderly woman was pushing it.

She wore clothes that were nothing more than rags and unfortunately smelled. Her hair was silver—what he could see of it, anyway, but he was unable to guess her age.

"Standing there in a towel, you don't look like you own much of nothing, especially not my alleyway."

Liam was about to argue with her when he realized just what she was looking at. He hitched the towel around his hips and took a step toward her.

She pulled a baseball bat out of her cart. "You stay back, you freak!"

"Whoa! I'm not trying to hurt you. I've already told you, I'm Liam and I really do own this hotel. What's your name?"

"My name's Jane. You don't look like you own the hotel."

"Listen, I do own it. If you tell the doorman around the corner to tell Travers I'm here, I'll give you a reward."

Jane shook her head and gave him a long look. "If I go to the doorman, he'll put me in jail and take Mr. Butterscotch. No, I have a better idea. You get out of my alley and take your crazy ways with you. I mean, you may own a hotel and all, but running around the city in a towel, wearing pink flip flops… Something ain't right with you."

Liam frowned and shook his head. Could this day get any weirder? Liam couldn't believe he was trying to prove his sanity to a homeless woman.

"Okay, okay." Liam hitched the towel again. "Let me just make sure the coast is clear."

Then it happened all at once: Mr. Butterscotch jumped from the cart and tried to grab the edge of Liam's towel; Jane shoved her cart and started to swing her bat; Liam ducked just in the nick of time as he picked up Mr. Butterscotch and tucked him under his arm.

"Don't hurt him," whispered Jane.

She looked genuinely frightened. Just when Liam was going to say something to her, Mr. Butterscotch started to give him kisses. He glanced at the dog to tell him to stop and then looked back at Jane, who was all smiles.

"Okay, I'll go to the doorman for you," she said.

Liam was dumbstruck, but managed to stammer, "Thanks."

"Keep your thanks. Mr. Butterscotch knows people, and if he likes you, then you're okay. I'm doing this for him, but it's gonna cost you."

"Fine. Just give the doorman the message," Liam muttered.

Liam pulled the towel closer, handed Mr. Butterscotch back, and waited for what seemed like forever. Every little noise made him jump and duck for cover behind a garbage bin. Finally, though, Travers, his dependable best buddy, showed up. He appeared a little skeptical, but when Liam stepped out from his hiding place, Travers shook his head and obviously tried to contain his laughter.

"Oh, I can't wait to hear what sweet little blonde left you like this," he said as he handed a robe to Liam.

"Did you bring shoes?"

Travers looked down and immediately pulled out his phone to take a picture. "I didn't, but as your best friend, I brought my phone to memorialize this new low you've set."

Liam pushed him aside, and with all the dignity he could muster, he walked into his hotel. Every step echoed from the flip flops hitting the marble floors; his best friend following behind him and taking pictures like a paparazzi photographer while giving colorful commentary; with his savior, Jane, the odorous homeless woman holding her dog, grumbling that she and Mr. Butterscotch weren't leaving without her reward.

Liam knew two things: he hadn't avoided making a spectacle of himself, and his grandmother was not going to be pleased.

Travers leaned against the bathroom doorjamb in Liam's hotel suite. "Dude, will you tell me what happened?"

"No one says *dude* anymore," Liam said, trying to get his friend to talk about anything else.

"Before today, I would have told you that the days of seeing your bare butt after a date were long over, but here we are. I wonder what other things are coming back around."

Before Liam could reply, a wet nose nudged his toes, followed by furtive licks. When he looked down, there was Mr. Butterscotch.

"Where's Jane?"

"Who?" Travers appeared confused. "Oh, yes, Jane. I

opened the door to the adjoining suite, and she is preparing a bath."

Liam smiled. "It's probably been a while since she's had one."

Travers snorted. "Um, Liam, she's running it for Mr. Butterscotch."

Just then, Jane called out, "Mr. Butterscotch!" The dog perked up his ears and then ran out of the room.

Liam looked into the bathroom mirror and saw his friend staring back at him.

"Liam, what happened?"

He tried to piece everything together. "It started with a call from Gran. She said that what I needed was a girl who could think. She said she understood that the other women she had tried to match me up with were all wrong for me and that I needed someone who would look past my lack of imagination and limited growth."

Travers had his hand over his mouth, but when Liam lifted his eyebrow and looked at his friend, Travers guffawed.

"Whoa. Are you telling me Gran called the hotel genius, and one of the most wanted billionaires in North America, boring and slow? That is so Gran! When I get older I'm going to be able to say anything—you hear me?—anything, just like her!"

Liam silently groaned. "May I continue?"

Travers settled against the doorjamb again. "Continue."

"So she told me there was a convention. There were a lot of college professors, I met this woman Sarah who told me it was a symposium, not a convention." When Travers looked a little confused Liam clarified.

"You know Sarah, the blonde that put me in this situation and the one I had to run from this morning?"

"Right. So what happened?"

"Sarah wanted to go for a walk. I said yes. I didn't like the crowd, either, and was relieved to get out of there. As we were walking, she said she felt ill. Her head was starting to pound, and it was the beginning of a bad migraine. She asked me if I would see her safely back to her hotel room."

Travers's eyes widened. "Tell me you didn't fall for that old trick? When in doubt, call a friend, man."

Liam looked back at his reflection in the mirror. His blue eyes were red, probably from the stress, his black hair was in such disarray that no amount of hand combing was going to fix it.

Call a friend, Travers had said. Nope, Liam hadn't even thought to call a friend, because Sarah was a non- threatening five foot three blonde, and he had become an expert in how to avoid uncomfortable situations. He had developed the skills to fend off gold diggers and potential blind dates his grandmother had tried to set him up with.

"When we got to Sarah's hotel, she could barely walk," he said. "She handed me her key to the room and pointed to the bedroom. Then she wouldn't move, saying she couldn't get to the bedroom herself and didn't want me to help her because I would wrinkle my jacket. I took it off and threw it over a chair. We got to the door and then she tripped me over her foot. I fell into the bedroom and she closed the door, locking me in."

Liam looked up. Travers, with his arms wrapped around his middle, was doing his best not to laugh.

"She had this all planned as she had already prepped the room by ensuring the windows were blocked. Realizing my phone was in my coat, I yelled, kicked the door and stomped my feet. Finally I heard someone come to the door, and it seemed like she apologized and told them I was emotionally disturbed, and these outburst could happen. The person outside said they understood but had just come to check on her to make sure everything was all right!"

Doubled over, Travers shook with laughter. When Liam stopped talking, Travers looked up with tears in his eyes. "Man, you have to tell me more."

"I asked her to let me out. She said she would if I undressed and put on a towel. I would have said yes to anything to be able to leave. After I undressed, she let me out of the room and then locked the bedroom with a key so I was unable to grab my clothes. So, I'm in the living room and she starts what she thinks is a normal conversation."

Travers held up his hand. "You can't skim over things like this. Inquiring minds want to know; did she make you do a strip tease? Does she watch – does she?"

"I heard the question! I didn't ask her if she was watching but I did see the camera in the room and I turned from it and threw my shirt over it so I wasn't flaunting the family jewels."

Travers sat on the rim of the tub trying to catch his breath after hearing that last remark. "What kind of conversation does a kidnapper have that's normal?"

"She told me everyone at the symposium had been expecting me. She said Gran had told them I'd make an appearance. She also said that Gran said I was looking for a wife, so she wanted us to spend some time alone together."

"Ahh."

"Then Sarah asked if I was a real billionaire or just a stocks-and-investment billionaire. I assured her I was a real billionaire with the cash and properties to match. I guess she wanted to make sure all the hassle of the kidnapping was going to be worth it. I suppose it must be a common problem for women to target men they thought were rich but turn out not to be. Anyway, by that time, I was fed up. I told her to give me back my clothes or I would leave in the towel, she said I wouldn't dare. I saw a pair of flip flops by the door so I grabbed them and then walked right out of her hotel. I walked the three blocks back here ending up in the alleyway where I ran into Jane and bribed her to go and get you."

Liam had just put on jeans and a blue top when the doorman showed up at the door, per Liam's request, and he thanked him with a hefty check. Once the door had closed, Travers continued his laughing.

"I want you to know, I think your experience was awful. It's horrible right now, but I have it on my phone, and later on, we will be able to laugh about it." Travers held his hands up and grinned. "Okay, okay, I can see you're not there yet, so let's deal with the problem at hand. Why does Gran keep sending these women, and why do you deal with it?"

Liam took a seat on the pearl-colored couch in the living room section of the suite.

"Travers, I've told you before, Granddad left me 49% of Butler Hotels. He left the remainder to Gran. Gran wants to give me the rest of it, but she wants to make sure work doesn't eat me up. She believes I need a woman, girlfriend, or preferably, a wife."

Travers waved the problem away. "Hire yourself an actress and then dump her."

Liam let out a breath before he spoke. "Been there and tried that several times. Gran always winds up separating us and then asking some odd questions that make it obvious we are not a couple. The last actress I had, I thought for sure would be a go. Gran was alone with her for twenty minutes before the woman came out crying, saying I was pond scum for trying to trick such a sweet woman like Gran."

Travers sat back on the pearl-colored love seat opposite the couch. "I didn't know your gran had those kinds of skills, that's impressive."

"Anyway, that's how I ended up here now."

"Your gran, as good as she is, is only one woman. Let's put our heads together and we will figure something out. We'd better get it done quickly, because we also need to pick a caterer for the opening of your new hotel," Travers said.

The door to the other suite opened, and with it came the smell Liam would forevermore associate with Jane. In her arms was Mr. Butterscotch, now fluffy and white. Jane gave Travers a look and then shook her head.

"If you need to figure something out, maybe you need another partner." Jane gestured to Liam. "The last time he thought he knew something, he wound up in an alley with Mr. Butterscotch and me."

CHAPTER TWO

Florida

Elissa Dane reviewed the red numbers that decorated her spreadsheet, making it look more like a cherry blossom painting than her catering business balance sheet, and let out a low moan. Here she was again sitting at her little computer desk as her Aunt Becky knits away cheerfully on the sofa. For once she was glad she hadn't invested in a large screen and just had to look at her shame on her thirteen inch monitor.

"Are you looking up some brand new recipes?" Aunt Becky asked. "You've been staring at that little screen all morning."

"I'm working on my financials for Green Magic."

"Well, that shouldn't take long," Aunt Becky muttered.

Elissa wanted to let her head fall down on the keyboard with the weight of that truth. Green Magic was failing. She'd taken a huge risk opening up a farm-to-table catering service in the nearby town of Chusada, Florida. Elissa had turned down a steady job offer. She'd taken money that should have gone to pay off her student loans and dropped it into a business investment instead. Like every newbie businessperson, she'd hired a couple of staff to do the day to day work and had loftily thought she would just have to manage orders. Chusada had other up-and-coming businesses: Moccasins, an organic shoe store that did well; and Nature's Nectar, a juice bar that always had a line. But Elissa's healthy, organic catering service had never taken off.

Aunt Becky came up behind her, tapped her on the shoulder and smiled at her. "You know, I have just the thing to make you happy; some banana pudding. I made it this morning. I can give you a bit before the Henderson's come by to pick up the rest."

Elissa just didn't get it. She couldn't even give her meals away to people to try, she had already tried. For Aunt Becky's pudding, the Henderson's were making a two-hour trip both ways.

"No, thank you, Auntie." Elissa smiled. "Unlike most people, food doesn't fix everything for me."

"Well, that's part of your problem right there. You have to enjoy life and have a fallback when things go south."

Elissa couldn't win this argument. Aunt Becky, a rotund woman who stood five foot two, could out-bake and out-cook anyone in the county, and she was a self-proclaimed *real woman*. Aunt Becky had real hips and enough cushion to make it through a bad winter.

Elissa, on the other hand, often wondered if she had been left on her parents' doorstep. She was five foot nine and had a runner's body and a child's metabolism. Whatever Elissa ate, she just burned it away. Elissa had long ago given up on waiting for hips like Aunt Becky's.

Her aunt pulled out the bowl of banana pudding and put it in a small dish on the table along with a serving spoon next to Elissa.

"I know you may only take a taste, Elissa, but at least I tried."

After closing her laptop, Elissa dipped half a spoon of banana pudding into her bowl. "I'm trying to figure all this out. You know it takes up to three years to get a business going…"

"Getting it going is one thing, but if this were a horse, we'd be waving the flies away from the body."

Elissa snorted. "Really, Auntie?"

Becky smiled. "You know I'm here for you, no matter what. I just don't know why you need to make all that fancy city food."

"It's healthy, Auntie. I've made it before and you liked it," Elissa reminded her.

"I did. I love that green kale—with some butter and salt and next to a steak."

Elissa laughed. "I have to find a way to make Green Magic successful. When I do, as I promised before, I'll give you the money back that you loaned me. That's why I'm interviewing in hotels and big cities." She needed to get the catering business going, or at the very least make enough money to give Aunt Becky back her investment. Her aunt had given her a considerable portion of her retirement nest egg. Elissa wouldn't leave her auntie out to dry. "Maybe all I need to do is build up a little reputation first, and then doors will start to open. I mean, the first thing people ask me is 'Where have you catered?'"

Aunt Becky snorted. "Don't forget, you did the Jansen's retirement party, and there must have been close to sixty people there. You did Paul and Jen's wedding, as well. I know it wasn't a big event, but they've been married and divorced four times now. We all figure if we miss one wedding, another will come up in five years."

As Elissa ate the pudding, the weight of just how much she hadn't accomplished made her head hang low.

"Did you tell the big city folks about those parties?"

Elissa let out a breath. "I did tell them. They asked for my references so I gave them the names and phone numbers."

"Well, then?"

"The problem is, all of the references said they thought I was a good caterer because they had seen the signs when I was growing up."

"We all know city folk are odd. I guess it's a good thing you're contacting those hotels in New York. That's what you said, right?"

"Yes, that's the plan."

"Did you contact Clara Butler's grandson who is working in the hotel business?"

The old heaviness of embarrassment came over Elissa. "His name is Liam, and yes, he is in the hotel business, but he's the CEO. I would be in the food and beverage department. I don't think he would be able to help me. Besides, I haven't spoken to Liam in so long, it would take a moment beyond desperation for me to ask him for anything."

"Surely you aren't still mad at him?"

"Why would I be upset that he agreed to go with me to

my college graduation dance on a dare? He was stuck-up and inconsiderate then, and I doubt he's had any reason to change. However, to answer your question, no, I'm not upset. I don't even think about it anymore."

But the truth was, the last couple of trips she'd made to New York, she had done nothing but think about it.

When she had gone to the Big Apple for the second-round interview, instead of being directed to a kitchen, she'd been shown into an office. Elissa had known, whatever they threw at her, she'd be able to cook. In her mind, the job had been a done deal. When she was instead led toward the administrative office, her apprehension had grown.

Finally, she'd been ushered into a room to find a reed-thin, but beautiful woman Elissa had suspected wasn't anatomically natural. Aunt Becky would have called her a toothpick. Her mane of hair had looked like Rapunzel's, which had explained why the woman's head had always been slightly bent to the side. On her best days, the woman had to have been a hundred pounds soaking wet and a size double zero.

A lovely woman had come into the room to explain that Elissa and the other woman whose name was Flora, were the finalists for the catering position, and they were both being evaluated for the job.

Aunt Becky, scooting into her chair at the table, brought Elissa back to the present. "Well, if we're not going to use our hometown connections, at least fill me in on what happened when you went to New York. You've been all closemouthed about it, and I've been waiting for you to tell me, but it's been three days, and that's long enough to have a wake and bury a person. So spill it."

Elissa dug her spoon into the banana pudding. "The

hotel representatives are testing their options for the new hotel. Cooking isn't just cooking anymore, especially for a five star hotel."

"I don't know that I really understand how cooking doesn't stand on it's own but go on. It seems like I'm missing something, so tell me what they actually said."

"They said Flora and I were both talented cooks, but the person who got the job would also have to be... a public representative of the hotel."

"Public representative." Aunt Becky scowled. "You said your competition was a toothpick? If you can look through her, no one is going to believe she can cook a thing. You know what those executives need?"

Elissa smiled. "They need a real woman!" she and her aunt said in unison.

"Well, they didn't say that, Aunt Becky." Elissa looked down at the bit of pudding she had left and was so grateful. She had an overwhelming feeling of gratitude that cocooned her heart. Aunt Becky was the best. Never pointing out the potential for failure, she was supportive to the end. Elissa didn't know how yet, but she would make matters right for her aunt. "So what they did was take us aside and explain what the other candidate offered and why the choice had come down to us. They thought we were both imaginative in our plating and flavorful in our food choices. However, the caterer would be part of the ambiance and potentially the permanent go-to for the hotel chain, so they wanted to make sure the candidate was unique and appealed to a wide audience. So they want me to come up with a new menu along with some pictures to send them."

Aunt Becky downed the rest of her drink. "The menu and

pictures won't be a problem for you. It seems like you just need to do you and you'll win, no problem. Both of us are here, and you know the rule; If two agree, it's done. Now, the Johansen's are coming. Did I tell you how that happened?"

"No, Auntie." Wishing she could be as confident as her aunt, Elissa relaxed in her chair.

"Mr. Johansen has a brother, and he's staying with the Johansen's at their house. You know there's a problem there. I mean, a grown man living at his brother's house. He's over the age of thirty, so he must be unemployed or beyond cheap.

"Anyway, I saw him coming out of the minimart with the Johansen's. They introduced me, and he said his name is Clyde. What kind of name is Clyde? It's a robber's name, and that means no job."

"Did you ask him if he had a job?"

Her eyes wide, Aunt Becky looked at Elissa.

"Why would I do that and get all up in that man's business? I'm not that kind of woman."

Trying to stop the smile from showing on her face, Elissa nodded. "Of course. Sorry."

"Well, after the introduction, he says to me, 'My brother says you make good pies and cakes.' I tell him, 'Yes, I do.' Then he says, 'Would you mind baking a couple for me and maybe a banana pudding?' I told him, 'You think I bake for just anyone?' I mean, baking for a single man, I might as well tell the whole town there is something going on between us. Then he says he'll come and pick them up, and I step back and say, 'Listen up. We're talking about baking for sure, and I live with my niece, so I'll deliver the goods to you outside when you come with your family.' He stepped back, and I laughed at him as I walked away." She sniffed. "I admit he looked all refined and distinguished with that bit of gray at his temples and that six-foot-one height, but I'm not that kind of woman."

Before her aunt had finished, Elissa was laughing. On schedule, Aunt Becky went into the sitting room to turn on the television to watch the morning news. Elissa put the pudding away then gathered her bowl and spoon to wash and dry them.

Aunt Becky gestured to the TV. "Seems like this week was rough on everyone in New York."

"Is that what we're calling it when our whole lives are hanging in the balance? What else happened?"

Aunt Becky cackled. "We were just talking about the Butler boy. We must have conjured him up, because someone got a picture of him walking in a robe and pink flip flops next to what looks like a bag lady with a dog. The news headline read: 'The Wild Billionaire Strikes Again with His Outlandish Taste in Women and Parties.'"

Liam. They said a man could work an outfit, but he was working that robe. The picture showed him looking over his shoulder. The robe had parted with his movement and revealed well-defined chest muscles that matched his sculpted calves, showing below the hem of the robe. His footwear would have made another man look foolish, but Liam had enough confidence and swagger to wear pink flip flops and still resemble a male in his prime.

He still had thick, dark hair that curled around his ears and piercing blue eyes that she had gotten lost in while he talked about his plan to follow his grandfather into the hotel business. She had thought he was sharing his goals and dreams with her; instead, he'd just been trying to win a bet. Taking a seat, Elissa got the remote and turned up the volume on the television.

"Local Chusadite Liam Butler has once again been seen in a scandalous position. Still to be determined are the events of him walking into one of his flagship hotels wearing pink flip flops and a robe with what appears to be a homeless woman, but everyone agrees, that regardless of the reason, his behavior is erratic at best. This type of speculation couldn't come at a worse time for Butler. Sources say he has been trying to introduce innovative approaches to keep the family-owned hotel chain above water."

The picture on the screen changed to an image of Liam's grandparents, holding hands and smiling at one another. The photo made Elissa's breath catch. Such love shone in their eyes, and their hands were entwined as if they were making a vow to one another.

"Butler was named CEO after his grandfather passed away a year ago. The transition affected the company's stock, as Butler made decisions that some stockholders saw as impulsive and lacking long term planning. It's been rumored that the board has asked for some concessions from Butler to show his stability, which is believed to be the reason for his seemingly endless pursuit of a significant other. A source, who wished to remain anonymous, said these public antics only confirmed that Butler may not be the CEO the company needs."

Elissa couldn't believe it. She was so shocked her hand tightened on the remote. She'd just been at that hotel in New York. Could Liam mess up her life again? She stood, clasped her hands together, and bent her head. If she took deep breaths and centered herself, she wouldn't explode. All she could see were the wasted dollars on hotel, plane, taxi fare and quick food that cost a month's worth of groceries. All of that spent for nothing.

"Elissa, are you praying?"

Her eyes flew open. When she saw her aunt's concern, she smiled.

"I'm sorry, Auntie. I thought Liam could use all the prayer he could get."

Aunt Becky agreed.

When the doorbell caught them both unawares, Aunt Becky stood. "I'll—"

"I'll get it. It's about time for you to go to the garden, yes?"

Her aunt nodded. "Thanks. Let me know if it's that Johansen guy. I mean, he can wait a little. It would do him good." Aunt Becky left the room with a little more pep in her step. It wasn't much, but whatever brought her joy, Elissa tried to provide it. The bell rang again, and this time, a knock followed right after. Someone was persistent.

"Hold on." It was probably not Mr. Johansen, but a local with another petition. It seemed like the neighborhood was overrun with petition workers.

Elissa opened the door and found herself facing a familiar man, but couldn't recall where she'd seen him before. She should remember a man who was so nice to look at, and most important of all, didn't seem to be at the door for a survey or to sell her something. If he was here to sell her something dressed in his business casual wear, she couldn't wait to hear his offer. He didn't have a clipboard, pamphlets, or a vacuum cleaner. If nothing else, she was about to hear a pitch she hadn't heard before.

"Yes?" she prompted.

He nodded and started patting his pockets as if he were searching for something. Elissa began to think he was lost and needed directions. He held up one hand and then let out a sigh of relief when he pulled out a bent, slightly crinkled business card . He handed it to her.

"Elissa Dane, my name is Travers Warner. I—"

"How do you know my name?" Elissa gave him a skeptical look.

"Sorry, we know each other. Sort of—"

"Sort of? I don't think so, Mr. Warner. Now, I'm not sure why you're here, but you can just—"

"And you thought I would make a mess of it," Liam said as he stepped into view.

Suddenly, Elissa was back in time, waiting for Liam to come to her door and say the rumors weren't true, that she wasn't a dare that he'd taken up. In truth, she had rehearsed this meeting many times. She had practiced saying how she hadn't wanted to date him anyway. She'd even had daydreams about him coming back and telling her how much he cared for her and was sorry, and she would just walk away saying, "Too bad, you missed your chance." All of those witty words left her. Now that she was face to face with him again, her mind had gone blank.

"Liam, I just wanted to introduce the situation first, and see if Ms. Dane was interested." Travers sounded exasperated , as if nothing he said or did mattered.

"I'm sure she'll be interested, so let's move past the formalities."

"Liam?" she asked. What was he doing on her doorstep? With yesterday's memory in her mind, she wanted to just slam the door and say it didn't matter why he was here. While her feelings were all for it, the part of her brain that calculated her budget and had already counted this hotel job as a win cautioned her to do otherwise.

"Hello, Elissa. I need to talk to you."

"What?"

Liam took a deep breath. "I hope you know how to do more than ask questions; otherwise, this could be harder than I thought."

"What are you talking about?"

"I'm talking about our marriage."

CHAPTER THREE

Elissa Dane had grown up.

Liam had both dreaded and craved this moment. Elissa Dane had been his nemesis in college. If he said right, she would promote left. The first two years of college, it had been Elissa vs. Liam, and then one day, they'd clicked—or so he had thought.

Today, she appeared to be everything he'd thought she would become: confident, beautiful, bold, and headstrong. In the morning sun, her dark hair shone. She wore it in a sloppy knot that could compete with any magazine model's. She had on a white shirt that was open at the top and showed off tanned skin. Elissa wore shorts that made her legs seem to go on forever. If he wasn't sure whether the rebel still lurked in her, he could see it personified in her bright red flip flops that matched her toenail polish. He suddenly had a new appreciation for women in flip flops.

One of her feet tapped the ground. When he glanced up, he looked right into her stormy eyes.

He recognized that ember of awareness in her gaze. Some things may have changed since they had last seen each other. Time may have passed, Elissa Dane may have filled out in all the right places, but one thing that hadn't changed was he still got a thrill seeing her rise to the moment.

If memory served him correctly, Elissa did not share his excitement. Her expression went from confused to indignant to full-on defensive. If he had to classify the transformation, he'd say it was changing from the playful debates they'd had to looking at him as if he were a snake. Definitely not a look he was used to getting from women. Considering the way she used to look at him in their last year in college, it definitely wasn't one he was used to getting from her.

"Did you just say marriage? *Our* marriage? Anything would be preferable to marrying you!" Elissa eyed Travers, as if by association, he was on the low list. "I remember you, Travers. You were his shadow in college, right? I'm sorry life didn't turn out better for you. Now, if you will excuse me—"

Travers stepped forward. "Elissa, please. I'd like to have a few words with you, at your convenience, of course."

"You know, Travers, you seem like a nice guy. That baffles me, because you're here with him. I don't have time for more college pranks from grown men. Marriage? Ha!"

Travers put his foot in the doorway and placed his hand on the door. "I'd just like a few moments."

"Uh, Travers, you might want to move your foot," Liam said.

His friend looked at him as if he were crazy and then back

at Elissa. She'd cocked her head to the side and was eyeing Travers's foot as if it were the new enemy.

"I'm sure Elissa and I can talk this over," Travers said in his confident I-can-handle-it voice as Liam took several steps back.

"We certainly can. Can you wait here for one moment?" Elissa said with a sweetness that sent off warning bells in Liam's head

"Of course."

Elissa walked out of view, and Travers glanced over his shoulder and winked at Liam. Less than a minute later, she came back to the door with a twelve gauge shotgun. With the butt of the gun, she smashed Travers's foot. Travers gave a howl of pain and hopped back. Liam barely moved out of the way in time, and Elissa turned the shotgun, so her finger hovered over the trigger.

"Travers, this is your warning. I was feeling very threatened by your foot being in my doorway, and I've taken some action against it. However, if you say the wrong thing, I may once again feel threatened and have to fire a warning shot into your leg. Do you understand what I am saying?"

"Liam?!" Travers whispered slowly.

Elissa turned her gaze to Liam. "He's asking for assistance. Are you going to leave him hanging, too? That seems to be your signature move," she quipped.

Liam gave her another long look. "I don't remember you being this… this…"

"Bold? Aggressive? Blunt? Well, these things happen when you have life problems that you have to fix on your own without the benefit of money."

Elissa turned to Travers. " You see how this is all about

him? Should I shoot him now, Travers, and get it over with? It's morning, so the nearby doctor should be in his office. Otherwise, Liam will have to go to the hospital. It'll be a wait, but they'll get to him."

Travers held his hands up. "Can we come up with a solution that doesn't call for me being shot?"

"Liam, I think you should teach him some manners about where he should and shouldn't put his feet at a woman's door. If you don't, he'll get you and himself killed." She cradled the shotgun in her right arm. "I like your gran, so you should try not to upset her by dying."

Elissa turned her gaze to Travers, who was dusting off his shoes.

"Ms. Dane, I apologize. I was rude, but we do need to talk about a proposal that might work for both you and Liam."

"Romeo here said *marriage*. I can't imagine a time when marrying Liam would be a good idea. I have problems already." She looked at Liam and shook her head. "According to the media, you can't seem to get anyone to stay with you, much less marry you. It's a big red flag when no one wants to marry a man with gobs of money."

Before Liam could speak, Travers did.

"Ms. Dane, we understand this wasn't the best time or approach. We'd like to talk about the caterer position you applied for, as well as a possible deal. There are some pressing time constraints. Is there somewhere you'd be more comfortable talking so we could discuss this matter in full?"

Liam had to give it to Elissa. She had managed to do what many a person in New York had tried and failed to do: make Travers retreat and negotiate.

"I can see you're a little slow, Mr. Warner." She looked at the card he had given her. "My trigger finger is getting heavy, and I can't think of a thing you could say that would be worth my time."

Liam held up his hands and took a step toward her. "Let me put this another way. How about if this deal helped you out with Green Magic?"

CHAPTER FOUR

Liam knew!

As the shame of her failing business hit her, Elissa had to lean against the doorjamb for support. She clenched her teeth and straightened her spine. Danes didn't bend. She needed to keep Travers and Liam away from Aunt Becky and definitely move them before the Johansen's arrived.

Just as she contemplated getting a shot off in front of Liam's foot, she saw her best friend, Colleen Bowers, her red ponytail swinging side to side. It was bound to happen that a neighbor would notice Elissa standing in her front door with a shotgun. If it had to be someone, Colleen, a beautiful six feet of lean and curvaceous muscle, was the best choice. Her legs ate up the sidewalk, and she took what seemed like three steps to get to Elissa's walkway.

In a pink workout shirt that said, "Real girls can think all by themselves" and dark blue running pants, she confused people on what to expect to come from her mouth. Elissa, on the other hand, knew. For the first time since answering her door her anxiety was starting to drop. Everything would be okay.

"Hello, everyone. Elissa, what's going on?" Colleen didn't even pause as she faced the men. "I'm Colleen Bowers, a concerned friend first and attorney if needed." Colleen's gaze went to the shotgun, then back to Travers and Liam. "I think you boys better start talking before I call the police on the obvious harassment going on here."

"Long time no see, Colleen," Liam said.

Elissa frowned. Had he lost his mind? He and Colleen didn't get along. The current situation wasn't going to help at all.

"It hasn't been long enough," Colleen replied. "Now, what are you two doing here besides harassing Elissa?"

"Ms. Bowers, I'm Travers Warner, COO of Butler Hotels." He held out his hand. Colleen didn't take it. "I'm sure you are aware of the very unflattering story about Liam in the Chusada paper today. After looking at all of the facts and some unique crossovers, we wanted to present Ms. Dane with an opportunity that would be mutually beneficial."

Colleen slowly clapped twice. "You said all of that with a straight face. Whatever Liam's paying, you ask for more, because you're good. To answer your question, yes, I did see him on the news today." Colleen turned to Liam. "By the way, pink isn't your color. Don't be stressed; it's a hard color to pull off. Try a deeper red. It'll complement your hair. Or even try something in the blue family to make your eyes pop."

"Thank you for the advice. The next time a woman steals my clothes, and I have to make do, I'll ask to see her whole collection before I escape."

Elissa looked at him in disbelief. "A woman stole your clothes?"

"Yes, and these kinds of things happen all too often when women want to marry your wallet and you happen to come with the wallet, as well."

"Well, you must have been doing something if she got you out of your clothes," Elissa murmured.

"She tricked me in to walking her to her hotel, then tripped me and locked me in her bedroom. I tried to escape. I yelled and kicked the door, but when help showed up she made up some story about me being off my meds. Stripping was the only way she would open the door. Listen, I wasn't doing anything wrong. In fact, I was trying to help her and had my clothes stolen for my efforts!"

Colleen looked at Elissa, and both of them started laughing. Elissa had to step into the house to put the shotgun away before she accidentally shot someone while laughing. When she came back, Liam's face looked red with embarrassment. He shrugged and then the right side of his mouth lifted into a grin. Travers and Colleen looked as though they were still trying to hold in their laughter. Elissa stepped entirely out of the house and leaned against the door.

What was she going to do? Liam's grin was like bait to her. It said he wasn't so bad, even though her head was saying he definitely was.

Colleen stood up to her full height and looked Travers in the eye. "It seems as though Mr. Butler has problems that are beyond the present company to fix."

Travers smiled and wagged his finger in the air. "No, no, no, you're an attorney, so you know we can't take these things at face value. In this seemingly disjointed telling, I think there can be some middle ground. Liam currently has an issue with women throwing themselves at his feet. The women are being encouraged by his grandmother in an attempt to find him a wife."

"You've got your gran scouting for women for you?" Elissa asked, horrified.

"No," Liam snapped. "She's doing it all on her own."

Colleen turned a sweet smile on Liam.

"I couldn't think of a person more deserving."

"Travers!" Liam prodded.

Travers turned to Colleen. "Like I was saying earlier, we have a solution. We understand that Ms. Dane has applied for the position of caterer for the launch of our new hotel. We are also aware she has a failing business that needs the revenue and exposure we can offer. We wanted to make a deal."

"He was making an offer, and I promptly got my shotgun to let him know I didn't take kindly to the offer," Elissa said indignantly.

"You have such a unique spin on things, Mr. Warner. I'm sure it's a result of you living in New York City. You and your boss intrude on her property. You don't make your intentions clear, and you threaten her by trying to forcibly enter her home, to the point she had to defend herself with a shotgun. You may be a COO in New York, but your negotiation skills need a brush-up, or you need to be taught some along with some manners." Colleen turned, pulled Elissa into her arms, and glared at Liam. "Mr. Warner can get a pass because he's not from here, but you, Liam? I'm surprised you'd let Mr. Warner come here with his high handed techniques. Were you going to let him bully Elissa into whatever it is you wanted?"

Liam's jaw tightened, and he held his hands out, effectively admitting to the plan. Elissa shook her head. Once a snake, always a snake.

"You may have a point, Ms. Bowers," Travers said with a sly smile. "Since this deal involves Ms. Dane's business, maybe Ms. Dane needs an accountant to help her understand what we are offering?"

Colleen's smile in return was just as smooth. "Mr. Warner, if you high-powered chief executives thought it would take two of you to negotiate a deal with a woman who has, as you say, a failing business, then me being in the picture really evens the playing field. I mean, at this rate, maybe it puts the two of you at too much of a disadvantage," she concluded sweetly.

Travers covered his mouth to cough, but Elissa swore he hid a laugh.

"If you will avoid dying in front of her house, can you tell us what you are offering?"

Travers nodded. "We want Elissa Dane to agree to marry Liam Butler in name only. There is a board meeting coming up. After the board members see he's settled down and married, they will confer the rest of the business to him. Once that has been completed, Ms. Dane and Mr. Butler will divorce. She will get the opportunity to cater to the hotel's grand opening. Green Magic will garner excellent reviews, and she will also be paid generously for the event—enough to address any shortages Green Magic may experience for the next two years."

Liam shook his head. "We could have gone to the market and hawked me like a piece of meat for all this deal is turning out to be," he muttered.

Colleen looked both men over and then let out a sigh. "Gentlemen, first, go wait by your car, standing here in front of Ms. Dane's house is causing an undue ruckus on her block and bringing unwanted attention from her neighbors. Ms. Dane needs to calm down, and we will be with you shortly —"

"Wait one moment." Elissa ran into the house, came back out with two water bottles, and handed them to the men. "Here, while you're waiting."

Travers took the plastic bottles from Elissa and nodded to her and Colleen before heading down the walkway. Liam followed.

"Hey, what are you doing? The way you're acting, Travers, I would think we're here for Match.com face to face."

Travers gave a deep sigh. "It's not my fault that my job brings me in contact with hot women like Colleen. I'm trying to foster relations between us is all."

Liam looked skyward. Fostering good relations between him and Elissa was just what he didn't need. He needed to keep this on a business level so they could easily divorce when he finally had the other fifty-one percent of his hotel.

"If you don't mind me asking, why is there more than a little tension between you and those two women?"

Liam and Travers leaned against the car and waited under the shade of a nearby tree.

"Colleen and Elissa have been best friends forever," Liam said. "Let's just say if I did anything to put Elissa's nose out of joint, then Colleen was offended, too."

"Ahh, dedicated to her friends. I tell you, I'm liking this woman more and more with all that I find out about her. By tonight, I'll know everything there is to know about Colleen, but at first look, she's looking pretty good."

"I think it's great that you're looking, but remember, we're here to save everything I own. We are not here to find you your one and only love."

Travers laughed. "Tell me, Liam, what do you think those two women are in there doing right now?"

Liam looked toward the house. "I think Colleen is planning with Elissa how to sell my story to cause the most amount of embarrassment."

Travers tsked, tsked him. "That's why I'm the COO, and you're the CEO. You look at the dream and the vision, but I look at what's going on right now. If I had to place a bet, I would bet that Colleen is in there right now trying to make sure that her friend gets the most money possible from this deal."

"You think that's a good thing?"

Travers held open his hands. "I think if she's willing to do that for her friend, we're dealing with a person who has some kind of emotional compass. Feelings I can appease. Greed? We'd have to cut a deal with an army of lawyers in tow. Come on, let's lean against the car like we were the original Miami Vice."

Liam winced. "Nobody knows that show anymore."

Travers nudged him over so he could lean on the car. "Never say nobody," Travers said with a laugh. "You knew it."

CHAPTER FIVE

"It's a shame time has been so good to that man," Colleen said. "Why is it that the bad guys always seem to look the best and get the best toys? And as far as sidekicks go, that Travers isn't bad at all."

Elissa could always count on Colleen being true to form. If there wasn't so much riding on the negotiations, she might even have sat down and indulged Colleen and asked her some more questions about what she thought about Liam's sidekick.

"Gorgeous guys are a sign to everyone that there's something wrong you can't see. That's why they're so good looking, so you get dazzled by the outside before you find out the character flaw on the inside." Elissa heard her words, and for a moment, had to think if she was really that bitter over the whole event.

"Hey, don't take that tone. Remember, like calls to like. So if Liam is gorgeous, know that you are down-right beautiful."

"Well, thanks, but right now, I'm just feeling down and out." Elissa moaned and took a seat in the kitchen. Colleen peeked around the corner as though hesitant to follow her.

"Aunt Becky is out in the backyard, you can come in safely," Elissa said with a smile. Colleen liked to shock people. But one of the things she would never do is offend Aunt Becky. While Colleen's outfit said that she was into fitness, Aunt Becky would look at it and tell her the reason she's having a problem getting a man is because she's not wearing man staying clothing, just man visiting clothing.

Elissa reached across the kitchen table and placed her hands on Colleen's. "I'm so happy you came over to help me."

"Well, I had to, because my roommate was talking about how she needed to throw on some clothing to try to catch the eyes of some random eligible bachelors on the block. Let's face it, that could only be but so many men in this town."

"Thank you so much for coming."

"Hey, maybe I should be insulted? Did you think a billionaire would stop me from coming to my best friend's aid? Besides, I could tell by looking at his sidekick that you were going to need some help."

"It seems like you could tell a whole lot about that sidekick, Colleen."

The red-haired woman sniffed. "Don't try and change the subject."

"Colleen, what am I going to do?"

"Well, let's make sure we understand all of our options."

Elissa nodded and waited expectantly for her friend to outline the situation.

Colleen held up one perfectly manicured nail. "One: Outside is a billionaire who wants to marry you. Two: He intends to give you money so you can save your business. Three: The only thing you have to do in order to get one and two is to lie to everybody you know in town. Well, I think that about sums it up. We'll have to go out there and tell them thank you, but no thank you."

"I thought you were trying to help me. Why am I going to go and tell them no?"

Colleen reached out and placed her hands on Elissa's cheeks. She smiled indulgently into Elissa's eyes. "You're going to have to say no because you, my friend, can't lie. Every time you get ready to lie, you have a tell: you tuck your hair behind your ear. Everybody knows the tell, and when we were younger, it was just cute. Now that we're adults, you don't usually lie, so it's no problem, but when you think you need to lie and I see the tell, I know there's a problem. So you getting married and trying to convince someone it's a love match is not going to happen."

Elissa sat back and blinked away the tears burning behind her eyes. "Aunt Becky invested almost all of her retirement into Green Magic. I've got to find a way to make this business work, if for no other reason than to give her back her money. I don't want to be why she has to go back to work."

Colleen looked shocked. Elissa waited for her expression to change to disappointment. Her friend sat motionless for all of ten seconds. Then she let out a large sigh, smiled, and looked Elissa in the eye.

"Well, that just means we are about to go and agree you'll get married to Mr. Billionaire."

"What about my tells?" Elissa asked.

"Don't worry. Being a lawyer, I have gone through years of school to learn how to lie efficiently and effectively. I'm going to get you through this. We're just going to work on some other things you can do instead of tucking your hair behind your ear."

"Other things?" Elissa asked skeptically.

"Yes, like… I strongly suggest you take up the habit of chewing gum. It may be the only thing that helps us right away."

"Do you really think that will work?"

"Do you remember when I asked you if you thought I could make it to law school?"

Elissa nodded, knowing where Colleen was going with this question.

"You told me, of course, and that you would be with me every step of the way. You told me that's what best friends do for each other. Do I think we're going to be able to get you through this? Of course, together, we will get you married, get your debt paid off, get Aunt Becky her money back, and then get your divorce. With the money left over, you can just start over. I will be here for you every step of the way. Do you know why?"

Elissa smiled. "Yeah, I do know why; because that's what best friends do for each other."

"Great. Now that all of the mushy stuff is done, I need you to tell me if there's anything else I should know about this situation before we go back out there."

"I don't think so," Elissa said as she tucked hair around her ear. As soon as her hand was on its way to her lap, she let out a frustrated sigh. "Oh, my goodness. It's true."

"Now, can we stop with the stalling? There is something, so spill it."

"Do you remember why I went to New York this past week?"

"You were going to look into a catering job at a hotel. Oh no! Tell me it wasn't his hotel."

Elissa nodded. "It was not only his, but a job I thought I had because it was a second interview. It turned out the position wasn't mine, after all. When I arrived, the selection process had changed."

"Ouch!"

Elissa nodded, letting the disappointment settle on her shoulders once again.

"I was so sure I had the job. At the first interview, the guy who was interviewing me said it was just a formality for me to get the position. Then, when I walked into the room, it wasn't to go into a kitchen and cook, like I had been told. Instead, in the room was a beautiful and statuesque woman; her name was Flora."

"So, she got the job?" Colleen asked.

"No. It seems the board members of the hotel decided that Liam's vision for a caterer was too progressive. They ran around the block to say they weren't sure if I fit their public image."

"Those sleazy snakes!"

"I was so disappointed and embarrassed."

"So they brought you to New York just to tell you, you don't have the job?"

"No, they brought me out there to say I could compete against Flora for the position. They gave us two weeks, and we have to come back with a fresh menu that is representative of the Butler Hotels."

"Why did you accept the offer to redo the menu?"

Elissa shrugged. "I thought it was the only way I could get Aunt Becky's money back.

"Then on the way out, Flora stopped to talk to me. Flora told me that the interviewer told her this was going to be a comparison of traditional values versus a fresh look. "

"I could give her something traditional all right. Maybe Flora wasn't telling you the truth?" Colleen tapped her nails on the kitchen table.

"No, I've heard it before at other venues. I don't think she needed to lie or would have been that swift of thought. Colleen, what am I going to do?"

"It's a yes or no decision," Liam muttered to himself. "What's taking so long?"

Travers was already on the phone, talking to operations about some issues that had come up. That left Liam leaning against the car and waiting. Waiting was one of the few things he wasn't good at.

Liam looked at the streets and remembered growing up here. Three girls caught his eye. It looked like they were all talking and about to play jump rope, but then one of the girls shook her head and walked away. It sounded like the two girls called out to the third one, but she didn't turn back. The two who were left appeared to be friends, and one put their arm around the other while they dragged their rope behind them. When they noticed him at the car, they stopped and then one smiled.

"I saw you on TV. You're Grandma Butler's grandson," the girl said as if she had just guessed the winning lottery numbers. It had been a long time since someone hadn't called Liam by name and had identified him by his family.

"I am," he replied. "How are you two doing?"

"We were going to play Double Dutch, but our friend left," said the girl wistfully. She wore her hair in a high ponytail, blue jeans, and a polo shirt with so much sparkle and glitter on it, Liam couldn't even read the words.

The other girl, who had her hair in pigtails, looked up at Liam.

"Do you think that you are balanced?" the smaller girl in pigtails asked.

Liam was at a loss. "Balanced?"

The ponytail girl nodded. "You are so smart," she said to the pigtail girl. Then the ponytail girl took one end of the rope and gave it to Liam.

"Okay, if you are balanced, then we can jump rope. Our friend said we weren't balanced so she couldn't play with us, but we can show you, and then we can jump rope," she said excitedly.

Liam looked over his shoulder to see Travers on the other side of the car. Travers smiled, waved him on, and then vigorously pointed to the phone at his ear and walked away. Since his friend wasn't going to help, Liam turned to the girls, thought why not and nodded. "I don't think I'll be any good at this," he warned.

The ponytail girl smiled. "Don't worry. I saw you on television. Everybody who wears Peppa pink can do this."

"Peppa?" Liam asked. The girl in pigtails started laughing.

"Peppa the pig. Everyone knows that. You are so silly."

Liam felt a lot of things right at the moment, but he couldn't believe his competence was being judged on him having worn something the same color as a pig. Thank goodness the shoes were the only thing she mentioned. He wasn't ready to have a modified talk with a girl.

"Okay, let's go!" ponytail girl said.

Liam hoped to see Elissa and Colleen coming out of the house, but to no avail. He did the only thing he could do. He smiled and began turning the rope.

"Okay, we are doing singles now. When you get that, we'll show you how to do Double Dutch, okay?" the ponytail girl told him. Liam nodded. Surely Elissa and Colleen would be ready to talk before that, right?

"You have got to see this," Colleen said.

Elissa walked over to the window facing the front yard. Outside, Liam was turning a jump rope for two girls. How could this man be such a Jekyll and Hyde when it came to his actions? He had to have some redeeming qualities if he was playing jump rope with the kids outside.

"How do you think they got him to do that?" Colleen mused.

Elissa sighed. "They didn't have to do much. That is just Liam."

Colleen snapped her fingers and closed the curtain.

"Hey, hey, let's not go looking for the good in the bad guy. Remember?"

Elissa went back to her seat. "That's the problem with Liam. He's not all bad. He adores children. He goes to events and mentors. I know he gives to charities. He doesn't just give money. He gives time. He once told me he wished he'd had more people to give him confidence when he was growing up. He said he only had expectations, but was never confident."

Liam had told her those things the same day they had volunteered in a soup kitchen for families. She had thought then he was the kind of man she wanted to marry and build a life with—before he'd betrayed her with the bet. The old cliché really was true: be careful what you wish for.

CHAPTER SIX

An agitated Travers came around the car once he was off of the phone. The ponytail girl saw him and looked between Liam and Travers. Liam would look every so often at the house. What would Elissa think if she saw him turning rope?

"Hello. Are you his friend?" ponytail girl asked.

Travers nodded and then tried to step around her. When she moved to block him, he stopped and raised his eyebrows at her. "Yes, young lady?"

"I'm thinking I'd like to jump rope with my friend. Your friend is turning one end, so I want to know if you'll be a good friend and turn the other?"

Liam had to smile as Travers took a step back.

"Your luck with women today is going downhill," Liam joked.

Travers bent down to be at eye-level with the girl. "How about we make a deal?"

The little girl shook her head, her ponytail swinging from left to right. "No deal. You're a stranger."

"But you just asked me to turn the rope," Travers said.

The girl sighed and folded her hands over her chest. "That's okay, because Grandma Butler's grandson is here and he is helping me, and you are his friend."

"Ahhh," Travers said.

He stood up and eyed Liam. "Can you step away from your friends?" he asked in a tight voice.

Just then, Liam heard the melodic tunes of the ice cream truck. Both girls looked at the truck and then sighed. Travers grinned.

"Little lady, I think Liam wants you to get some ice cream while he talks to me for a minute. Is that okay?"

The girls looked at one another, and then Liam was faced with two eager children. He smiled and then reached into his pocket to pull out a couple of bills.

"How is it that I'm doing this?" he muttered to Travers.

"Because they're your friends," Travers said with a smile. A moment later, the cash had been transferred, the girls had left, and Liam looked at Travers.

"This day has been a total miss so far." Liam couldn't hold back his frustration. "We came here to offer a deal to Elissa that you said any woman would take. We run into Colleen, who happens to be the town's pit bull lawyer, and now I've been conned by two cute little girls who first pushed me to help them jump rope and then got money from me. This is not what you said we were doing. Tell me when this gets better."

"Well, it's not going to. We need to have a conversation that neither one of us will like," Travers said grimly.

"What now?"

"I just got a tip-off that the board is seriously looking into giving you a co-chair. They think you are too radical. They plan on approaching your grandmother and recommending a person they will pitch as being a good figure for you to follow."

"You're sure?"

"The executive assistant and I go back." Travers cleared his throat. "We've got to change some plans."

"How much of a change, and what are the board members actually complaining about?"

"Liam, they say you are making too many changes in the staff, and are upgrading the equipment in the hotels too fast."

"I make sure everyone keeps their job! I put everyone in training and ask them where else they would like to work if the new position doesn't suit them. We have a three percent turnover rate in the hotel."

"I know you see these as good things, and they are, but they are happening too soon for the board. The person they are looking at is someone they know. Someone who has a ten-year plan on how to modernize the hotel as opposed to your eighteen-month plan."

"Fine, they're nervous. I get that. That's how the marriage to Elissa will help. I'll have the marriage certificate, and they'll see me working in the hotel, and I'll be a stable person. Done."

Travers gave him a side-eye look.

"Why are you looking at me like that? I'm giving you what you want."

"No, Liam, you're not. I don't think you can fake your way out of this situation."

"Fake my way? I'm here!" Liam pushed away from the car and ran his hand through his hair.

"You're here, but I think you're going to have to stay here until the board meeting."

Liam stared at his friend. What was Travers saying, to leave New York City? Liam had left this town for a reason. Besides, New York had a beat and a rhythm to it. Chusada had a pulse, a very steady one and if you stayed long enough you began to move to that same predictable pulse. Not happening.

"Yes?" Travers asked.

"I'm waiting for the rest of the joke," Liam said.

"No joke. You have to put in some face time and genuine effort to make your relationship with Elissa look real."

Liam thought about the hotel and how he loved it. Every day he met new people and learned new ways to give guests an enjoyable experience. It was a passion for him; a gift from his grandfather. His grandmother's intentions, although good, could cause Liam to lose all that was important to him. "Travers, tell me what to do. I'll get married, but will I still have the hotels to run?"

Travers nodded. "You'll need to stay married until the board meeting. If you get engaged here in town, your grandmother will get word of it. It seems like everyone knows everyone's business here," he muttered.

"How will you get Elissa to agree to this plan?"

Travers smiled. "You have money. You have a lot of money, so I'll get her to agree. She wants to keep her business, so cash is already on the table."

"Not everyone wants money, Travers, and I'd think Colleen would want to clean house, not Elissa. You may not even get to Elissa if you can't be nice to Colleen. I'm telling you, the red-head is her protector for life."

Travers gave Liam the smile he often used right before sealing a deal. "Don't you worry about her lawyer friend. I can handle her."

Liam laughed. "Many a man said that while we were in college. I'm surprised you didn't meet Colleen then."

"I had no time for women in college. You know I had to pull two jobs and do classes."

Liam nodded. "I remember waking you up in classes the next day, as well."

Travers smiled. "If I can survive that, then surviving Colleen and Elissa will be a cinch."

"This is a nice place," Travers exclaimed. They had made their way to the park at the side of the church. People were going in and out of the building. Elissa had to admit she felt a lot calmer being here. But, Travers didn't seem to share her sentiment as they sat on the picnic benches.

"What's wrong, city boy?" Colleen teased. "Been so long since you've been on church grounds, you're not sure if you'll go up in flames?"

Travers shook his head and found a place where everyone could sit down.

Elissa sat, shut her eyes, and absorbed the afternoon sunlight. This is what she needed; to just sit here and relax. The church grounds were always well manicured, and the grass smell never went away because the gardeners cut the lawns every day. Aunt Becky had brought her to these grounds as a child and had told her she could do anything she put her mind to.

Elissa could stay like this forever, but she knew she had to come back to reality and try to figure out the whole mess with Liam. As she opened her eyes, what she was hearing finally dawned on her. "You can't be serious!"

"I realize what we've proposed may be an inconvenience for you, Elissa. We are willing to look at that," Travers said.

"An inconvenience? I can't believe you even made that suggestion on church grounds!" Elissa said.

As if seeking some help, Travers turned to Colleen. "Hopefully, you can see how this isn't as bad as it seems?"

"Not as bad as it seems?" Elissa asked. "Are you for real? You want us to fake being a happily married couple." Her having to pretend to marry Liam was one thing. If they did anything more than pretend to have a genuine relationship, she would have to share her life with him.

Again, Travers talked directly to Colleen. "Miss Bowers, surely you can see some upside to this? Things happen very quickly in the business world. It turns out the best thing for Liam and the Butler Hotels would be a marriage that, outwardly at least, appears to be sincere."

"Things do happen very fast, Mr. Warner, and not just in the business world," Colleen replied. "You came to Chusada, and you really don't understand how quickly information travels in a small town. I'm not saying we will agree to your proposal, but I do want to hear what the terms are."

Travers smiled and then leaned a little closer toward Colleen.

Elissa placed her hand on her friend's arm. "You really want to listen to this?"

Colleen smiled. "My love, I want to listen to everything

before I can advise you on what you should and shouldn't accept."

"I knew there was something about you that I liked," Travers said.

"Don't get too happy," Colleen cautioned. "I'm just finding out all of her options. Nothing more."

"We were transparent and told you our reasons for making the proposal. It appears that the board members have become a little more critical of Liam, and we want to dispel their concerns."

"Ah, I see. You mean, you really need to make sure Liam looks married because otherwise, your board members won't buy it," Colleen said.

Travers shifted in his seat. "That is an accurate interpretation of the situation."

Colleen leaned back and then held her hands open on the table. "I do sympathize with your issue. The problem is, it's detrimental to Elissa to stay married to Liam. She has to live in this town after he's gone. As it stands, we would like to stay with the original agreement. We are sorry for the other problems Liam has, but this is as much as we can do."

Just then, someone tapped Elissa on her shoulder. It took everything in Elissa not to jump. She turned to see an older lady dressed in her Sunday best: a yellow dress that went all the way down to her mid calves and a matching white bonnet.

"Hello, Sister Clara," Elissa said.

"Hello, dear. I didn't expect to see you. What are you doing out here? I believe I saw your Aunt Becky go inside. Are you planning to attend the Bible study?"

"No, but I will go into the church to check on my aunt. Thank you so much." Elissa looked at Travers and Colleen going back and forth over the same details. In truth, Elissa thought they looked entirely too happy.

She glanced over at Liam, who was standing and walking away from the group. He had his cell phone to his ear and appeared to be totally engrossed in the conversation. Whatever was being discussed at the table obviously hadn't moved him. Elissa gave all the parties one more look then got up and went to the church to check on her aunt.

No one would notice she was gone.

CHAPTER SEVEN

For the first time, everybody seemed to notice every step Elissa took.

She walked toward the church, and a family waved to her and called her name. She waved back. When she got closer, she recognized one of the children she taught bible class to on Wednesday nights. As Elissa stepped into the vestibule of the church, other matrons called out and gave her a hug. Then she saw Sister Clara again.

"You children are so fast. I just got into this building. You know, at my age, you'd rather be sure than quick."

Elissa smiled and looked around. "Sister Clara, have you seen my aunt?"

"Oh, yes, oh, yes. I did see her. She got a call and needed to take it alone. Look in the pastor's office. You'll find her there."

While Elissa was on her way to the pastor's office, her cell phone rang. She thought about not answering the call, but saw the New York area code and realized it was the interviewer from the hotel.

"Hello?"

"Ms. Dane, how are you?" the manager said brightly.

"I'm fine," Elissa said tremulously. This was the last person she'd expected to call, and she definitely couldn't take any more bad news right now.

"It seems there are some questions we perhaps neglected to ask you."

"Oh?"

"Yes, Ms. Dane. Do you happen to know anyone in the Butler Hotels?"

If she hadn't been standing in a church, Elissa was sure she would have sworn. She walked to the side, so she wasn't taking up the hallway.

"I'm sorry, I didn't see that question in the interview paperwork, but yes, I do. I know both Mrs. Butler and Liam Butler."

"Ah. Well, it's not a deal-breaker, but we've decided to review the applications as you can imagine," he laughed nervously.

"I didn't mention it because I didn't want to cause any undue stress or pressure," Elissa said, shaking her head and pulling that errant curl around her ear.

The manager laughed. "I appreciate your sense of fairness. Have you seen Mr. Butler?"

"He's outside. Do you want me to get him?"

"No, no, it's as we thought. We are sorry for the misunderstanding, and we will be reviewing the materials you've already submitted."

"Umm, I don't want to be nosy or anything, but how did you know to call me?"

The manager stayed silent for a moment. "We… Well, on the news just moments ago, Mr. Butler was reported to be outside of your house. To be candid, Ms. Dane, the reporter said that after a wild night and showing up in disrepair at his hotel, Mr. Butler went to stay with an old college sweetheart to recuperate and rest. The question right now is if he is resting or if something more is going on."

"Oh, I'm… we're…"

"It's okay, Ms. Dane. I didn't call to find out the answer to that question. I just called to let you know that your affiliation was not known, and it will be put into the mix appropriately."

"How does it affect the final decision between Flora and me?"

"That isn't known yet, but I will keep you informed."

"Certainly, and thank you for calling."

Elissa tapped the screen and looked at her cell. Running back to his college sweetheart. Someone in town was already making a dollar off of her. That culprit would probably be found in the next day or two.

It galled her that the manager didn't care about her food or the effort she put into making healthy creations. Her stomach churned as she thought about how she might have to adjust to these new circumstances. She didn't want to get the job because management intended to make Liam happy. She shook off those thoughts. She would make sure her aunt was okay and then go back to Liam and the dueling duo.

The church had been newly renovated. Elissa walked to the end of the hall and almost missed the doorway until she saw a door protruding from the wall. The pastor's office had previously been in the basement, but now the whole hallway looked like a single panel of wood until a door opened.

Elissa put a smile on her face and reached for the door to look inside when she heard her aunt's voice. The words chilled Elissa.

"How many hours do you think I could get? They explained it will be more supervisory, and the pay won't be a lot, but it's okay. I'm not looking for full-time yet."

Seconds went by, but they felt like hours to Elissa. There was a mountain of guilt that weighed her down and threatened to crush her. "Yes, I did see Sister Mary last week. She was the one who gave me the number for this."

At seventy-two years old, Sister Mary had never married, had no kids, and had no one to take care of her. People gave her jobs so she could earn extra money. She'd worked as the town seamstress for years, but her business had gone under when her health had started to fail. Sister Mary's situation showed the benefits of living in a town that had known you all of your life. When hardship struck, everyone was there for you.

"Thank you for helping me out and managing to keep it low key." Aunt Becky's nervous tone made Elissa's heart clench. "If at all possible, I don't want it to be public knowledge. It's a good job and a fair wage for what I'm doing. I just need to ease into it."

Elissa put her hand to her mouth to stop a gasp on its way out. She looked over her shoulder to make sure no one was coming down the hall to witness her blatant eavesdropping.

"I've managed to refinance most of the items and put myself on a budget until I can build up my monthly payout."

Payout?

"I know my retirement fund payment is smaller after the loan. Yes, I thought it would be back also, but I have to say, I'm not concerned. I didn't really understand when I took the lien that I wouldn't get my regular amount back then, but it's okay. I built it up once, and I can do it again. Thanks for all of your help."

Elissa peered through the crack in the door to see her aunt sitting with her head hanging low and both of her hands braced on the pastor's desk.

Her aunt put up a hand. "Lord, you've gotten me this far. I know you won't leave me as I go forward. I praise your name in and out of the storms."

Elissa stepped away from the door and looked up at the ceiling. What had she done? She'd been so wrapped up in herself that she had forgotten anyone else. She had to make this right. She turned from the door and went back to the side exit of the church. A sense of purpose defined her strides as she walked. She was going to fix this mess right here, right now, and she knew just the person who was going to help her.

How had Elissa moved so fast? One moment they had all been in the park. Liam had noticed one of the church women talking to Elissa. He'd taken a business call, and when he'd looked back, Elissa had been gone. He'd experienced a little panic, thinking Travers and Colleen were talking for nothing without her, and then he'd seen her coming from the side of the church. He didn't know why, but the sight of her had calmed him.

Something about her was different. Elissa's back was stiff and she walked as if she were going to war. He wanted to tap Travers on the shoulder, but Elissa's demeanor made him decide to take care of her himself.

He hoped there weren't any problems with the women in the church. He knew how prim some people could be, especially in a small town. Elissa stopped in front of him and just looked at him. With the sunlight on her hair, her face lit up and in that moment he saw that woman he had fallen for before. She was strong, beautiful and confident. If all of this history and baggage wasn't between them, he could see himself falling all over again.

"Elissa?"

"I know what I need to stay married to you."

The statement made him take a step back as if she had slapped him.

"Yes?"

"I'll need money up front."

Liam heard the words, but he couldn't believe them. "Elissa, what—?"

She held up her hand. "I don't want to discuss it. Can you give me the money up front?"

Disappointment weighed him down. Then Travers's words about everyone having a price came to him, and he realized once again, he'd been naïve about women and people in general.

"How much do you want?" His tone had turned brusque. Elissa flinched, and he didn't give in to the urge to make her more comfortable. She probably only saw him as an endless supply of cash anyway. This was a woman who had told everyone in college that he wasn't the one because he wasn't smart enough. People didn't change, and he just had to get that through this head.

"I need eighty thousand," she said.

"I didn't know that was the going price to stay with me. Don't you think that's a little low to compensate you for your time?" Again, she flinched. Determined that he wouldn't feel any guilt or shame for his words, Liam turned away from her to look at Travers.

"This is hard enough for us both, Liam," she said. "Can you do it?"

Liam laughed bitterly. "I can. Let's go tell —"

"Hold on. There are some things we need to discuss besides the money."

Liam turned around and laughed. "Oh, was there something more important than the cash here? I'm surprised."

"Maybe we should stop before we start. If you're going to act like that, there's no way we are going to convince anyone we are happily married."

"Fine. What else would you like?"

"No one must know about the money but us."

"You don't want anyone else to know how well you made out?"

"Liam, it's not about me. It's about Aunt Becky. I don't want her to be embarrassed." There it was again that flash of the woman he thought Elissa was, kind and considerate about other people. Not a gold digger at all.

Liam sighed and nodded. "Done. I have my own conditions."

Elissa's head picked up. "You have conditions? I'm marrying you. I think that's all you should get!"

"Well, you're not marrying me for free, so let's not pretend you are doing a public service sacrifice."

"Fine. Go ahead. What do you want?"

"I want to be the one to decide how long the marriage is. I mean, I want to make sure I get my money's worth."

"If this is your attitude, I'm not surprised you need to pay for a wife."

He gritted his teeth. He wouldn't feel bad; Elissa was the one charging him. "I want six months with a review and we'll stay at the hotel."

Elissa laughed. "Whoa there! I guess this is you making real the expression give a man a rope, and he thinks he's a cowboy."

"What's the problem?" Liam asked, aggravated.

"The problem is, I have a life. I know you have a life, as well, but you can move yours here to Chusada. I can't move mine to New York."

"You want me to stay here? In this town?"

"Yes, I do. What's wrong with that? Is the town not good enough for you anymore? Your grandmother is here."

Liam ran his hands through his hair. The negotiations were all going sideways. All the women in his life were just wrecking it. At least his grandmother cared about him. Elissa? He didn't even know what had happened to her, but they were close to a deal, and he couldn't quit now.

"Fine. Six months with the opportunity to review and we can stay here."

"Done." Elissa's shoulders lowered in relief.

"Well then, let's go and stop the dueling duo over there and then get the paperwork done. Because it looks like, Mrs. Butler, we have to find us a house."

CHAPTER EIGHT

Elissa studied Liam sitting across from her at the kitchen table at her house. Aunt Becky liked to say Elissa had a habit of expecting the worst. Elissa hoped her aunt wasn't right.

She and Liam had told Colleen and Travers about the agreement. Colleen had been shocked, and Elissa expected a phone call from her about the issue. Travers, on the other hand, had seemed triumphant. While Liam had been surprised when she'd said her terms, he was the last person who should be judging. Who messes up to the point they need to buy a bride?

"What are you thinking, and why are we still here? Shouldn't we be looking at real estate listings?" Liam asked.

If the man could just not talk, he'd be so much more attractive.

"Umm, do you really want me to answer any of those questions?"

"Yes, I do. We're going to be together for a while, and I'm not a psychic. I think we should be as open as possible."

"Okay, well, we're waiting for Aunt Becky to arrive. She needs to see you before I can leave and find a place with you."

Liam's brows rose. "Are you serious?"

Elissa rolled her eyes. "I am. I hope you remember that we do things a certain way, the proper way here in Chusada."

"More like the backward way," he muttered. "You want to stay here instead of a luxury five star hotel. I still can't believe it."

Elissa slapped the table and Liam's head popped up.

"Let me be clear about how this is going to work. The people in Chusada are my family. Maybe you've forgotten but they're your family, too. That means if you are going to stay in this town while you get yourself out of hot water, then you'd better remember the rules and fall in line. People are always more important."

"Are they more important than eighty thousand dollars?"

She was going to knock him on the head, roll him in the living room carpet and then dump it over a cliff. Yes, that would work. She closed her eyes and took a deep breath.

"If you are going to make it through this supposed wedding, you're going to have to get on board!"

Liam held his hands out. "I'm here, aren't I?"

Elissa could feel a migraine coming on. She just had to make it through the rest of the day.

"First, you need to say sir and ma'am."

"What?"

"Remember where you are. Shake off your New York City views and think like a Chusadan. You're new, and it would be rude if you didn't. We need to make sure we get all the clearances from your grandmother and my aunt and –"

"Hold up! We're not in high school. You do remember I run a company that makes its shareholders millions and employs thousands of workers?"

Elissa smiled as she leaned across the table. "That might be true, but right now, our marriage is the only thing that's going to save all of that. So I suggest you remember what it's like to be humble so you can survive the moment."

"I'm humble! People think I'm charming."

Elissa snorted. "Hmm, we'll see."

The front door opened. Elissa stood up and waited for Liam to stand. She cleared her throat.

"Yes?"

"Get up! You're supposed to go first," she hissed.

"It's your house."

"You go first in case there's an intruder. You'll get hit first." Was he really such a simpleton?

Liam looked confused, but he stood up and went to the door.

"Hello?" Colleen called out. When Elissa stepped from behind Liam, the red-head's smile grew wider.

"I see I got here just in the nick of time. This whole situation is looking good, Elissa. He came to the door first; good touch. Now, confess to your friend. You had to tell him to do that, didn't you?"

Smiling, Elissa nodded.

Liam looked at them both. "Why are you here, Colleen? Do I need Travers?"

"Oh, puh-lease. I practically live here," Colleen said. "Aunt Becky and company are on the way. I wanted to give you a heads-up."

"And company?" Liam asked.

Elissa turned to him and nodded. "It won't be that bad. They just want to come in and make sure you're a good person."

"I don't know who's coming in, but she's riding with the sisters," Colleen said.

"The sisters?" Liam asked.

"Women of the church. Just make sure to talk louder when they're here," Elissa said. "Some of them are a little hard of hearing."

"Really? Do we really have to do this?" he moaned.

Colleen smiled. "This is only the beginning. I think you've been away from home a lot longer than I thought, Liam. I also think you two should come outside and meet them—so you can meet them and go."

"Good idea. Go out, and we'll be right there," Elissa said. Colleen hesitated and then left.

"I wasn't going to be mean to Colleen," Liam growled.

"It wasn't even a thought. I want to talk about words you can and can't say."

"Words?" Liam appeared confused. "I think you may be taking this a bit far. I talk to my grandmother all the time. She doesn't have a problem with the way I talk."

"That was when you were a single man on the loose, and no one had told you better. You were sowing your wild oats and the such."

"Sowing my wild oats? I'm not that old!"

"Exactly what is 'not that old?'" Elissa asked.

"I'm in my late thirties, okay?"

Elissa grimaced. "Wow, you are old."

"What?"

"I mean, you have money and you aren't hard to look at. But, you don't have a wife or partner. It makes a person think something has got to be wrong with you. Just so we can cover the basics; do you have any diseases?"

"No."

"Any bad or illegal habits like alcohol or drugs?"

"No. I don't put that stuff in my body!"

"Good, good. Do you have any ex-wives, girlfriends, or children?"

"No, no, and definitely no. I realize no one will believe me, but I spend all of my time running a hotel chain and ensuring it makes money."

Elissa held out her hands. "Don't get testy, I'm just asking, and I won't be the last one."

Liam pouted. "Can we go now?"

"No, we have to do words and signals."

"Tell me you're joking."

Elissa smoothed her shirt, and as she headed to the door she said, "I'm not joking. You can't tell a lie or say any curse words."

"Lie? If you don't lie down, what do you do? Float?"

"Lie as in tell a lie. You can say fib."

"Is fib even a word?"

"It is for you," she said. "Remember, no cursing."

"I got that one."

"Good. If you say something or begin to talk about an inappropriate subject, we will have a code word: sparrow."

"A code word for inappropriate– Listen, I can make sure nothing inappropriate comes out of my mouth."

Before Elissa could reply, Colleen stuck her head back in. "Time to go, people! What's the code word?"

"Sparrow," Elissa said. Colleen nodded.

"I live in a civilized world. I won't need that word."

Elissa looked at him doubtfully. "I'm hoping so. Now, let's get out there."

She had just closed the door behind them when she saw Aunt Becky coming up the lane and the sisters waving goodbye as they continued on. A small measure of relief coursed through Elissa's body. Aunt Becky loved her and would do anything for her. This was actually the best scenario there could be in this situation.

When Aunt Becky got to the walkway, she stopped and looked Liam up and down.

"So, you're Clara's grandkid?" she asked.

Liam glanced at Elissa, who nodded. He took a step forward and extended his hand.

"Yes, ma'am. She's my grandmother," he said with a smile. Aunt Becky looked down at the hand, took a step forward, and then kneed him in the groin. Liam went down, and Elissa's aunt walked right around him.

"Welcome to the family. I'll be back. I need to get some water before I hear this story."

CHAPTER NINE

Liam couldn't remember the last time he had been sent to his knees. No one in their right mind would do such a thing to him.

"Are you okay?" Elissa asked.

All sorts of answers came to his mind, but he couldn't articulate a single one of them. Liam didn't know what was worse: the initial hit or the recovery as blood flooded everywhere, making it torture to try to move and agony to stay on the ground. Pride made him grit his teeth and push himself up. He was seeing the world through a filter of sparkles and colored spots, but at least he could breathe.

"The good news is, he didn't wear those skinny jeans that are all the rage. If he had, he wouldn't be able to move this quickly," Colleen said. Even her expression had a shred of sympathy.

He pushed up, and Elissa guided him to a chair on the

porch. A few moments later, Aunt Becky took a seat in front of them.

"I was at the church today. You do know where the church is, Mr. Butler?"

Liam nodded. Then Elissa's foot nudged his. The pain the light gesture generated made him grit his teeth.

"Yes, ma'am. I do."

"Good, good. It bodes well for you that you know where the house of the Lord is. Anyway, as I was saying, I was at the church. When I arrived, some strangers were there. Now, it's true we are growing as a town, but you usually see the city folk in the diner or in the quaint dessert shop. You don't ever see them in the church. I wanted to assist them, so you know what I asked?"

Liam had regained the ability to move the right half of his body. The left side still throbbed, but he was slowly making it to an upright sitting position. When he looked over at Aunt Becky, one of her eyebrows rose, and for a moment, he was scared she'd knee him again.

"What did you ask, ma'am?"

Aunt Becky smiled. "Well, what I asked was, 'You there, nice gentleman. Why are you here?' He said he wanted to see the woman who he thought had finally managed to tame the wild billionaire and bring him to the altar. Now you know this is Chusada. There ain't a whole lot of possibilities for who that woman could be."

"No, ma'am."

"But I'm thinking to myself, 'Self, that can't be, because if such a thing had happened, he would have presented himself to me all proper like.'"

Liam heard her voice building like a train gathering speed.

This wasn't going to end well for him. He couldn't believe he was here in his hometown, and while Liam had prepared to face all types of businesspeople, he was being schooled by one of Gran's friends. He couldn't even imagine what would happen when Gran found out he was getting married.

"Ma'am, I was coming to–"

"Oh, my goodness. Look at that sparrow!" Elissa said.

Aunt Becky gave her a look and Elissa became obsessed with her hands in her lap. Her aunt might not be wearing a corporate suit, but he could see she would be able to give the sharks a couple of lessons on how to control the masses.

"Now, where was I? Oh, yes, we were about to hear you try and lie to me?"

Liam heard her voice gathering momentum, and his leg unconsciously shifted to cover his crotch.

"Ma'am I wouldn't—"

"Are those baby sparrows on the ground?" Colleen called.

Aunt Becky turned to Colleen and then looked between Elissa and Colleen. "You two keep up that sparrow business and you'll find yourself in Sunday's choir singing about it since you are so obsessed with them."

"Excuse me, ma'am. Please let me start over." Liam stood up gingerly and then held out his hand. "I'm Liam Butler, Clara Butler's grandson and the man who'd like to marry your niece, Elissa."

Aunt Becky shook his hand. "It's a start. We have some talking to do before I go ahead and give you my baby."

"That is my cue. I'll be leaving now," Colleen said. "Elissa, Aunt Becky, have a good day. Liam, hopefully I'll see you around." She exited.

Hopefully, Elissa knew what was going on. It didn't matter.

Liam couldn't be distracted, because he had a feeling this was one parental meeting he might have wanted Travers to attend.

"I'm an open book. You can ask whatever you like," Liam said, trying to be accommodating.

"Yes, I'm sure you will tell me," Becky said.

Her tone reminded Liam of the evil witch in *The Wizard of Oz* saying "I'll get you and your little dog, too!"

"The first thing I need to know is, can you take care of Elissa?"

Liam let out a sigh of relief. He could answer that question with confidence. When he glanced over at Elissa, she didn't look as sure. She had just gotten him to sign over eighty thousand dollars!

"Ma'am, I'm a billionaire. I'm the CEO of Butler Hotels. I can take care of Elissa," he boasted.

"Is that true?" Becky leaned back in her chair. Liam gave his best press smile. Any moment she would begin the oohs and aahs that came after that kind of announcement.

They were dead! Liam thought his fake smile and saying he was a billionaire was going to be the Holy Grail, but Elissa knew better. While he believed he projected confidence, from this side of the fence, he looked like a snake-oil salesman who had come to the door and was selling the elixir to cure all things. He had a rakish smile. He was leaning to the side like those 1950s leading men projecting "maleness."

"Well, then, you won't mind telling me how much cash you have?" Aunt Becky's voice had a no-nonsense edge.

"Cash? I have assets—"

"No, I don't mean that fake money that is all digital. If the computers died, how much money do you have? Certainly, you have a safe. You can't be one of those people who keeps everything on some flimsy plastic card and hopes the cyber people out there don't steal from you? A man needs to have cash," she reiterated.

"Cash?" Liam said as if it were the first time he'd heard the word. Elissa had to do something, but still tell the truth, because she wouldn't lie to her aunt.

"Liam doesn't usually keep cash, but he just gave me some, and I have to get it from the bank," Elissa said.

Her aunt turned to her. "It's enough for you to take care of yourself on your own?"

"It's a good nest egg, Auntie." When Elissa thought about how her aunt had always been there for her, she had to hold back the tears. When Elissa had lost her mother, Auntie had never tried to replace her. She'd just wanted Elissa to know she was loved. Every Mother's Day, they went to her mom's grave. Aunt Becky would tell her stories of her mother, and they'd look at old photos. Elissa had checked her account an hour ago, and the money Liam had promised had been there. Aunt Becky had always watched over her and she would always be there for her aunt, as well.

Becky sat back with a smile on her face. She looked them both over. "Are you two sure? You're not rushing into marriage because there's a bun in the oven, are you?"

"We're sure, and there's no bun in this oven, Auntie."

Becky slapped her hands on her lap and stood up. "I don't know why you're in such a big rush to marry, but you kids always do things the hard way first. However, if you say you're good, that settles that then. Let me welcome you properly."

Elissa grabbed Liam's hand and they rose. He was still standing a bit crooked, so she guessed the pain hadn't entirely gone away.

Auntie hugged them both and then took a step back. "Well, then, it looks like we're all kin to one another."

"Thank you, ma'am," Liam said slowly.

"Like I said, that part is over. We need to address some things. First, those city folk at the church insinuated you had a very active social life, Liam."

He looked over at Elissa. She hoped he said the right thing because there was no way to call sparrow now.

"I can explain. Because I have money, women follow me. Also, Gran has been trying to get me settled this past year, so I've been dating more than normal."

Aunt Becky nodded. "I understand you're picky like my Elissa. That's a good match there." The older woman gave Liam another once-over. Elissa was glad they were standing. They could escape soon.

"Liam, what do you do?" Becky asked. So close to escaping, but not close enough.

"I'm sorry, ma'am. I run—"

"No, I know about your job. What do you do with your hands?"

"Nothing right now." Liam looked at Elissa and then back at her aunt. "I guess until I get myself squared away, I'll be helping Elissa with Green Magic."

"She'll be able to teach you. She has time. Let's talk about where you two will be living."

"Elissa and I are going to be looking for a place right–"

"There's no need. We can all stay together, I have two bedrooms upstairs, so it'll be a great opportunity for us all to get to know each other."

Aunt Becky gave Elissa one more hug and held on real tight. "Remember, I'm always in your corner," she said in her ear. With that, Becky walked inside and closed the door.

Elissa turned to look at Liam.

"I'm sorry, did your aunt say two bedrooms?"

CHAPTER TEN

The following day, neither he nor Elissa were in a good mood as they stepped onto his grandmother's porch. When Liam climbed the steps to the door, he winced with each step.

"You could have told me you weren't comfortable last night," Elissa said.

"I'm confused about how you thought I would be. It's a twin bed!"

"It's an extra tall twin bed," Elissa replied in a low voice.

"We'll have to find a place right away. Let's put on our game face here," Liam said. He knew Elissa wasn't happy, either. After he'd rolled out of the bed and found he was hurting in places he didn't think he could name, Liam had called Travers. This morning he'd driven Elissa Dane to a lawyer's office where they'd been married, and she'd officially become Elissa Butler. No church wedding for her Aunt to attend and preen, just a civil service and no frills.

He'd experienced a sense of triumph when he'd seen her name as Elissa Butler for the first time. He thought he would have felt trapped. He was still burnt over the money, but as time went on, he was seeing that maybe Elissa was just human and tempted like most people would be by cash. It was still at odds with the girl he'd known, but he was trying to find out the woman she'd become.

The door whipped open and Grandma Butler pulled Liam into her arms. She was homegrown from Chusada, but had found the love of her life on a trip to a museum. Grandpa Butler had fallen in love with her, and they'd decided they would make a home for everyone and Butler Hotels were created, or so the town story went.

Her gray hair was perfectly curled. She wore blue slacks and a white blouse with pretty eyelets around the collar. She was the epitome of delicacy and politeness. She was also the most important woman in Liam's life. Travers had wondered why Liam treated Gran with such kid gloves. The truth was, Liam owed all he was to her. Whatever she asked, he'd never say no. Hence, when the women had started pursuing him, he'd just dealt with them. If his dates hadn't gotten more aggressive, he might have let them go on, but that last one had given him the chills.

"Welcome home, Liam," his grandmother said with a smile. "Although I would have preferred you telling me you were here as opposed to learning from the news that you were in town."

"Gran, you know how the media folks are; they have no life." Quicker than he thought she could move, Gran turned, took a step toward Elissa, and grabbed her hands.

"It seems you are the woman of the hour. You look beautiful.

"Please, this is your home now, too, please come in, and please call me Clara."

"Gran, this is Elissa—"

"Dane. I know her, Liam. She's lived here her whole life."

"Well, she's a Butler now and you're the first to meet Mrs. Butler."

"Let's have tea. Liam will make it."

Liam's head popped up. Gran had kicked him out of the conversation. He hadn't expected that at all and quickly realized he should have. He'd thought he would come in and introduce Elissa and then leave. He hadn't counted on his grandmother taking a liking to Elissa right away. As he fixed the tea, he heard them talking.

"I'm so sorry you had to see the recent foolishness with Liam. You'd think people had something else to see rather than Liam running away from that woman. Now, with such a smart and attractive wife by his side, his old lifestyle will be behind him. Isn't that right, Liam?"

"Marriage does put a new view on the world."

Gran nodded and smiled. "I can't wait to let the church sisters know."

Liam smiled. "The church sisters?"

"Yes. The social structure is apparent, Liam, and big news like this is significant. The church sisters are the receptacle of all knowledge."

Elissa cleared her throat. "I'm afraid Aunt Becky might beat you to it."

Clara laughed as Liam brought them their tea.

"It's okay that Rebecca beat me this time. I'll make sure I know before anyone else when you two are having a baby."

Liam almost dropped the cup of tea he had poured for himself. When the hot liquid hit his hands, he yelped. "Ouch!"

"Liam, are you okay?" Gran looked concerned. Liam nodded and then waited for her to come and look at his hand. Instead, she gave him a smile and turned back to Elissa.

His wife must have seen his shocked expression. "Liam, are you all right? Do you need help?"

Before he could reply, his grandmother waved him off. "Elissa, don't be pulled in. He panicked and had that accident when I spoke about my future great grandchildren."

"We just got married a few hours ago, Gran," he muttered.

"You're getting up there in age, Liam. I heard stress can have an adverse effect on a man. One day he's conquering the world, and the next, his opportunity to have children is gone, worn away by stress."

"Gran, I'm good and I'm here!" Liam reminded her.

"Hmm. I didn't think you'd be so close-minded. Maybe you should go find something to do," Elissa said in a quiet voice.

Was she crazy? No way was he going to leave the two of them alone.

Liam caught the small smile on Elissa's face. He remembered that smile. She'd smiled that way when she'd met him after school at college; when she'd brought him lunch to his job when he'd been working. It was a smile he'd believed he knew. Then he thought about the money she'd taken and shook his head. The smile might be the same, but she wasn't the same woman.

"I am so glad that you're here, Elissa. Please don't be discouraged by what you hear about Liam. The only things he needs are some stability and someone who understands him."

Elissa and Liam's gazes met. He grumbled and then picked up his cup of tea.

"I don't think I'm really all that bad," he said.

His grandmother patted his hand.

"Of course, you don't think you're the problem. But I have to tell you, this year was a very trying one for me. I'm getting older, Liam, and I need to be sure you're okay. If it is at all possible, I want you to know the same kind of true love that your grandfather and I knew."

His grandmother focused on Elissa.

"I think we should get you out in public as soon as possible. We want to make sure everybody knows that Liam is no longer on the market. He has settled down and he is now a happily married man."

Liam tried to think of an excuse to prevent Gran from taking Elissa out and about on the town. The guilt he felt after hearing about Gran's love match weighed on him but he tried to reason it away by thinking of all of the people he would be helping by staying at the head of Butler Hotels.

"Clara, thank you so much for welcoming me into your family. I already know all about Liam's past with other women. I think the best thing, though, is for Liam and I to take some time to get used to one another. I'd like us to have some settling-in time before we make the rounds. The one place we are going to have to go today is the church. My aunt goes to that church, and I want to make sure there is no extra conversation or gossip."

Gran put her cup of tea down and then sat back in the kitchen chair. After a few moments of her looking at Elissa, she smiled.

"I'm so glad you said that. I know it doesn't sound very charitable, but for a moment I thought something wasn't quite right between you and Liam. I think you're going to be the best thing ever for him."

Liam had heard enough.

"It's so funny to me, Gran, that you think she is the best thing for me, but you have been trying to introduce me to so many women this year."

"Liam, do you know what I learned from your grandfather?"

Liam shook his head.

"I learned that men are very stubborn. You can tell them something that is for their own good, and most of the time, if it isn't their idea, they don't take your advice. They will have to try every single option before they come back to the right one, which more than likely is the one you said in the beginning."

Liam was a bit confused. "And you knew what the right option was all along, Gran? The next thing you'll be saying is that you knew Elissa and I would get together."

"I know a lot of things, Liam. Now the two of you need to move along. I don't want to interfere in your getting-to-know-each-other and settling-in time."

Liam stood up and gave his grandmother a kiss.

"You be good, Liam," she warned.

"What could go wrong when we're going to a church?" Liam said.

CHAPTER ELEVEN

Elissa decided they needed to stop by the house in order to freshen up to go by the church. It was the perfect time for Liam to reach out to Travers. Hopefully, his best friend had been able to get some information on the board members and who exactly was trying to get Liam out of his CEO position. While waiting for Elissa, he stood in front of the house and made the call.

"Travers Warner here. How can I help you?"

"Don't you ever look at your caller ID? Every time I call you, you answer like it's a business call."

"Liam, how are you? The reason it sounds like a business call is because this is a business phone. Why can't you call my personal cell?"

"Just calling to check-in, and this was the last number you called from."

"No problem. Not much has changed. I'm still waiting for some of my resources to get back to me."

Liam chuckled. "You are the only one in the company where that expression has two meanings. I'm not sure if you are going to meet someone at dinner, or you are taking someone to dinner."

"Don't criticize. It gets you results, and that's what matters. So how is it going?"

"It's going fine. Gran is in love with Elissa. Her aunt is a very straightforward woman. She actually kneed me in the middle of her front yard for not following protocol."

"Ouch!" Travers chuckled. "I guess she didn't knee you too hard, since you're still talking now."

"Let's just say I would love to have Elissa's aunt on our negotiation team."

"Seems like all is well. Are you going somewhere?"

"If I told you, you wouldn't believe me."

"You just got married to a woman you used to know because you're sure she dislikes you enough to divorce you. Simultaneously, we are trying to prevent a corporate takeover and find out who's encouraging the board to kick you out. I think I'm very open right now to anything you might say."

"I'm going to church."

Travers was silent for a moment, and then Liam heard laughter coming from the other end of the line.

"Okay, that was a good one. But really, where are you going?"

"This is something you don't know about small towns. I never really went to church when I was smaller. I was always with my grandfather at work, but the church is the happening spot. Besides, the truth of the matter is, Elissa teaches Sunday school there and her aunt frequents the church, and I was just on television, so we have to make sure her congregation sees

Elissa has not been corrupted by a foreign evil and that her Aunt Becky doesn't get any backlash from her marrying me."

"Oh. Huh."

"Yeah, yeah, yeah, there is no way to explain it. You just have to live it." Liam heard the clicking of what sounded like heels. "Listen, I have to go."

"Uh, Liam, I'm curious. Do you have church clothes on?"

"Sure. My clothes are clean."

Travers laughed again. "I think you've been away a lot longer than you think."

Liam looked at the phone as he heard the echoes of Travers laughing. He glanced up to see Elissa in a beautiful blue dress that belted at the waist, flared at the bottom, and accentuated how shapely her calves were. The look was topped off with the lowest heels he had seen on a woman under sixty.

He smiled, gave her a nod and a thumbs up. "You look great."

"Well, I wish I could say the same! Liam, why do you still have on your jeans?"

CHAPTER TWELVE

Funeral pants. That's what he was wearing; the pants he kept with him in case he had to go to a funeral. They were itchy. They were off the rack, and they were pinching him in places he didn't want to think about right now.

"Why did we have to walk again?"

"I know you don't expect us to drive everywhere, Liam. It's an unseasonably cool day and the church isn't that far, and we walked to it just the other day when Travers and Colleen were here."

"That was the day I wore jeans and could walk like a normal person."

"If all you're worried about is a little chafing, that's what coconut oil is for."

"We are officially approaching TMI."

Liam caught the look Elissa cast over her shoulder at him. Typically, he would have responded, but right now, he was just trying to make sure he could get to the church in one piece.

Out of the blue came the ringing of church bells.

"Oh, no. We've got to hurry," Elissa said in distress.

"What's the rush?"

"I was hoping to be able to go into the church while everybody was inside. The bells signal the end of the service. Everyone will be outside in the yard."

"Am I missing something here? Isn't that what you wanted? For everyone to see us?"

Elissa mumbled something under her breath. "I want them to see us. I just don't want them to ask us any questions."

As abruptly as they'd started, the bells ended. Elissa stopped and Liam almost ran into her.

"We're too late," Elissa said quietly. She'd stopped just a couple of feet away from the park by the church. Her shoulders slumped, and she had an air of defeat about her for some reason.

Liam saw nothing but women congregating outside the building. Elissa, though, probably saw a gathering of vultures.

"Elissa, this isn't a problem. I do press conferences all of the time. If I can tell a bunch of stockholders and investors they are not going to get their money back, I can go and talk to a bunch of church-going women."

"I don't know, Liam. Press conferences have rules. Maybe we should just come back tomorrow, and I'll have to tell Aunt Becky that we didn't make it."

Liam grabbed her hand and took her down the hill toward the crowd. Reluctantly she went with him.

The closer they got to the church, the less he understood Elissa's fears. The women seemed nice and to be helping one another. In fact, every place he looked, he saw nothing but smiling faces and helping hands. Elissa had to be blowing her concerns out of proportion. If anything, he'd have to watch his words to make sure he didn't hurt anyone's feelings.

"Don't worry. I've got this, Elissa." Liam felt like he was talking to a recruit fresh out of college. He'd often trained new college grads. "I know this must be intimidating for you, but remember, I do this all the time. They will probably just ask questions about why I was on television and not about us."

Elissa hadn't said a thing. They were too close now to the group for him to look to his side and make sure she was okay. Actually, that was rule number one: If you're going to face the mob, at least make sure you look confident, regardless of how you feel.

"If we get asked where we met," he added, "we will say we met at my New York hotel when you came to apply for a job. If they ask why we married so soon, we'll just say love at first sight."

"Love at first sight? Yeah, I can see how that's going to go really well with the 'wait and see what the spirit moves you to do' crowd. I'm curious, Liam. How successful are you at these press conferences?"

"My story sounds better than we got married to save your business and my corporation."

"When you put it like that, then yes, your story sounds great," Elissa said in a small voice.

"Lissa, look at me."

Elissa looked up and appeared to blink away unshed tears. "You haven't called me Lissa since college."

"Well, I'm sorry. I didn't mean to offend you."

"I'm not offended, but thank you."

The situation was odd, but also perfect.

Now he could definitely tell women were looking at them. This would have been the perfect setting to actually propose to her. If she had still been his Lissa.

"Listen, we have to make do in the situation that we have. We both have our reasons for doing what we're doing, and we need to hold on to those reasons to be able to make it through. Right now, those women down there are in our way. We're not going to let them throw away our plans, are we?"

"No, we're not."

"Then let's go, and I'll show you how it's done. All you need to do is stay by my side and every so often nod your head in agreement."

"Really?"

"It's exactly what happens when I'm doing a press conference for the company."

"Are you telling me they let you get in front of people and basically say you're right about everything, and they just nod and agree?"

Liam thought about her question and then nodded yes.

"Well, you should have told me you had planned on handling our marriage the same way. I would have gone out there and gotten you a horse and put a dress on it, and you two would have been just fine together, because you'd need something that would be obedient to you." She threw back her shoulders. "If that's true, I can so understand why the board is trying to get rid of you."

"*What?*"

"No one wants to be around someone who thinks they know everything." After saying that, she walked ahead of him and left him with his own thoughts. What was her problem? He was offering all of the best solutions he could think of.

If they didn't get a handle on this situation between them, it was going to ruin them.

An unnatural hush went through the garden.

He caught up to her, and she looped her arm through his, even though her body tightened up. It wasn't supposed to be this way, but he was rooting for her. This was a woman who did what had to be done. She didn't shy away from the mess, she ran right into it.

"Be gentle with them, Lissa. We are on church grounds," he murmured in her ear.

She looked up at him with a smile of relief and thanks. "I know how to act on church grounds."

How did he do it? One moment Liam was the embodiment of all that was bad in a person; then he turned a switch on or something and he became the most supportive person she had ever met. Right now, she needed him to take her mind off of things, and as if he had been watching her, he knew what to do. A man who could do that was one you could trust to be there for you. A man who was that attentive would be a best friend and a partner.

This thing between her and Liam, though, was a business deal and nothing else.

"Hey fighter, don't gaze too long into my eyes. The watching public will say we are having inappropriate eye contact."

She laughed and faced the crowd. "You're right, for once."

"Elissa," Joy Frost said, "so glad that you made it out

today. You know we weren't sure if you'd show up… at all. Now don't keep us all waiting. We've all heard of Liam, but I can't say I've been introduced to him."

Another woman showed up next to Joy, smiling. She waved her fingers at Liam. "Hello there," she said in a high-pitched voice. Elissa knew after the two had broken the ice, the rest would follow, and they did, like clockwork.

"Hello, Elissa."

"Nice to see you, Elissa."

Their comments were so fake, Elissa wondered how the sugary greetings didn't make their teeth rot out.

After enough people had politely gathered, Joy, the queen, took back the reins.

"I was just congratulating Elissa and her husband."

Elissa cleared her throat. "Thank you so much, all of you. Until you get a family, you know the church family is your first one. Everyone, please meet my husband, Liam Butler."

Liam nodded and smiled. Just when it looked like he was going to speak, Joy cut him off.

"Really, Elissa. I can't imagine what would make you get married without your church family being there? I know you haven't been around as much since that incident with the treasury and your Aunt Becky but family forgets and forgives you know."

Liam's arm tightened around Elissa's waist. He was there and she wasn't alone. It was empowering to be this force facing them all. Even with Liam there Elissa wanted to fall into the ground. How could Joy bring up that incident now? When money went missing from the treasury, her Aunt Becky had been the treasurer. Fortunately it was a small amount but for Joy to bring it up now, was just low. Elissa could only hope Liam wouldn't harp on it.

Elissa smiled brightly at Joy and hoped she wasn't squinting like the Mad Hatter.

"Well, you are my church family, but the good book says when you are going to marry, you must cleave to one another, and we felt that the time was right. We wanted to start anew and get a fresh coat of grace." Just then, Liam leaned in and placed a chaste kiss on her forehead.

The crowd tittered. Someone in the background said, "I would cleave to him, too, if he was my husband."

"Now that you are married, are you going to be leaving Chusada?" Joy asked.

Joy was like a dog with a bone. Elissa didn't really have an issue with the rest of the women. Joy always seemed to look for some way to make her look silly or foolish.

"No, Joy, I am not leaving town."

"Liam, you are a busy man. How do you think you will adjust to being home again?" Joy dug.

"Thank you, Joy, for asking. I have to say, it is a relief to be able to come back home. Listen, ladies, I don't want to interrupt your festivities. Elissa and I just came out for a bit of sun. May we sit at your table, Joy?"

The woman's chest puffed up; she liked being recognized. Elissa was going to have to tell Liam he was right. He knew how to figure out who was important in a crowd and then find a way to stroke their ego. Joy showed them to her table. Some of the women walked away and went back to their activities. However, when Elissa looked over at Joy, she could tell the woman was far from done.

Joy smiled like a shark right before it took a big bite.

"I'm so interested in how the two of you managed to finally get together. If memory serves me right, you were a couple at one point years ago, and then you broke up."

Elissa waved off the comment.

"You know, people have to let bygones be bygones. I went to an interview at Liam's hotel, and he happened to be there at the same time. Once we reconnected, it all started to fall into place."

Joy's expression turned to amused disbelief.

"I have to say, this sounds very familiar. Elissa, sometimes you can be impulsive. Like when you opened Green Magic. It was a great idea, but you needed to build it up more."

Elissa knew her smile had hardened. Joy had made her the center of attention, and the other women were leaning in and waiting to hear her answer. If she just pushed Joy onto the ground, would that give her enough satisfaction and distract everyone who would be waiting on her reply?

"I only bring this up because I am a part of your church family," Joy added. "It seems like you may have rushed into another business deal again."

CHAPTER THIRTEEN

Liam was getting better at reading his wife. With his arm around her waist, he felt her whole body tense up. That dig about Green Magic had hit too close to home.

Joy leaned back in her seat, and for a moment, Liam wished she would tumble over onto the grass behind her. The church family he and Elissa had come to see was as aggressive as any room of investors.

The longer Elissa took to reply to Joy, the more triumphant the woman looked. Joy was leaning on the picnic table and resting her head on her hands as she waited for the answer she was sure would never come from Elissa's lips. Like sharks that had smelled blood in the water, women had moved closer to the table and were sitting with their backs to Elissa, as if they were talking to someone else.

Liam had been determined to let her handle this problem. He might have been able to keep that promise if his arm had not been around her. Sitting next to her, Liam could feel the slight tremble of her right leg.

If he got involved now, getting the divorce would be a little more complicated. The other choice: to watch the women tear into her and leave her reputation in shreds? That just wasn't an option. At that moment, Liam decided they were in this together.

"Funny that you should bring up Green Magic, Joy," Liam said, shifting the focus of attention to him. "I recognized Green Magic as the brilliant idea it is. Of course, such an innovative idea needs to be in a big city. There just isn't a large enough client base here in Chusada." He pulled Elissa closer until her head rested on his shoulder. "We continued to talk while she was in New York, and I realized that this amazing woman who is so full of entrepreneurial spirit really was my match. My grandmother has also been eager for me to get married. I told her I would do it when I found the one. Little did I know the one was waiting for me here at home."

Liam let the words sink in. The women around the table, who had been pretending not to listen, were now fully engaged. The only one who didn't look happy was Joy. He decided to finish the matter off. He gazed down into Elissa's eyes. "I guess the saying 'home is where the heart is' is true."

His hand had been alternating between stroking her neck and twirling errant strands of her hair about his fingers. When he looked down at her face, he saw her eyes were partially closed, and her lips were trembling and beckoning him to take a taste of them.

Gone was the light in her eyes that said this was for the

crowd. Her hand came up to his shoulder. A kind of electric shock ran from her to him.

"That's right, Liam. Home is where the heart is," she murmured.

The crowd fell away, and it became just about them two.

"How could I resist a woman who is so like me? One who is compassionate enough to care about her aunt and stay in a town that can't really appreciate her? I look for opportunities to make deals. She didn't rush into this one. I was lucky she was willing to sign on early before someone else saw the treasure she is."

Liam was shocked to find himself enthralled with her on the lawn of a holy place, where being so close to a woman might have felt uncomfortable. Being with Elissa felt sacred and right. What was it about her that made everything he did seem like the first time? He lowered his head, and instead of just taking the kiss, he hovered above her lips. "May I?"

Her body melted into his and she nodded. He was glad she'd said yes. If she had said no, he would have pulled back.

His lips touched hers, beginning a slippery slope of perfections. Her heartbeat rushed in tandem with his. His breaths started to come quicker, and he needed to get closer to her. Just when he had placed a little more pressure on her back, Elissa pulled back and rested her forehead against his. "Liam, please," she whispered.

Her words were enough to bring him out of the moment, make him draw back and let their breaths mingle while they recuperated.

The kiss had just changed his world. He'd just had one of the most enthralling and meaningful kisses of his life, and it was with his wife.

The world had finally gone crazy. Elissa had read stories about a kiss being a game-changer, but until today, she hadn't known what those stories had been talking about. She wanted to say the kiss had only been a kiss; just a physical reaction to Liam. Truthfully, the kiss had been amazing, but the man had taken a step toward recovering her heart. Being in close proximity to him was already challenging. She was not immune to his intense gaze. He exuded an aura that said he would take care of her no matter what. All of those attributes she could have fought off, but when he'd whispered, "May I?," all of her defenses had come tumbling down.

His request had brought back memories of being with a man who she'd thought was going to be with her forever; of late nights in a little hole-in-the-wall restaurant where they'd both talked about their dreams. It had spoken of a time when she'd thought she'd known Liam, and she'd loved him. Their problems had all seemed inconsequential and like a blur. And after this kiss, she wasn't sure if anything that had happened was worth losing the feeling that had just graced her again.

As her breathing slowed, she reached up and traced her finger down his face. When her pointer finger reached his chin, she gave him a small tap and then smiled.

"Thank you," she whispered.

Elissa turned back to the crowd. Her face had to be all

kinds of shades of red. Still, she managed to look Joy in the eye.

"Forgive us, please," Elissa said. "We are still in the honeymoon phase." Several women around the table tittered and laughed, assuring her they totally understood.

The crowd around the table started to disperse, and Elissa wanted to call out to them to stay. What should she say after a kiss like that? Would Liam even bring it up?

Elissa didn't like being in a position where she didn't know what to do. Fortunately, fate was on her side. A crack of thunder sounded in the air, and everyone looked up to see clouds rolling in. Everyone on the lawn started to gather their possessions and go home. Elissa tapped Liam on the hand, and they, too, decided they would walk back home before the storm set in.

"I think that went well," Elissa said, keeping a steady pace for them to get to the house.

"I'd say it went somewhere, alright."

Elissa heard the critical tone in his voice. He was going to take what had been one of the most beautiful moments for her and destroy it.

"Thank you for going along and being so nice and civil in front of everyone, Liam. Green Magic wasn't something we had discussed, so I want you to know that I am grateful for the way you stepped in."

"I'm not an ogre, Elissa. I think we can still be humane to one another."

Humane? Is that what he'd thought about their kiss?

Not long ago, she'd seen him on television, running around in his robe. Their kiss probably had meant nothing to him.

"You seem quiet. No good comes for any man when a woman is quiet," Liam said.

"I guess you have a lot of experience of no good coming from women. That means you would have had to have a lot of women around. Listen, there is something I want to talk about. The next time we are out in public, you don't have to go ahead and touch me. Us sitting next to each other is just fine."

Liam's steps halted behind her. She didn't turn around. In fact, now that the words had left her mouth, she felt like the worst person ever.

"Listen, I didn't mean to offend you, Elissa. I'll make sure I stay away."

How had this happened? Why did she feel lower than low? She had to pull herself together. If she were honest, Liam hadn't done anything. The problem was, she was starting to feel things for him that she'd thought were long gone and dead. She couldn't let their relationship go on like this. She was going to be the bigger person and woman up. Elissa pivoted and Liam almost walked right into her.

"For the record, there was nothing wrong with your arm around my waist. I guess I'm always looking at people around me and waiting for someone to make some kind of judgment. You did the right thing, and you really came through today, and I want to thank you."

She didn't wait for his response. When they got to the house, she walked quickly into the home to avoid him seeing the truth on her face.

CHAPTER FOURTEEN

Elissa had just finished going over the new menu she intended to submit to Butler Hotels. The guy on the phone earlier had said she wouldn't have to do that, but it didn't seem right. This attack of conscience was obviously bleeding over from her shabby treatment of Liam earlier. She had holed up in the room for as long as she could. If she were honest, she preferred to do her menu planning outside. She was just trying to avoid Liam.

Taking a stretch, she decided to face the music and go outdoors. If she saw Liam, she saw him. Just when she was ready to step outside, her cellphone rang and it said: 'Just keep swimming. Just keep swimming.' Colleen had picked out the ringtone after they'd seen a movie, and it was so appropriate for her.

"Hello, Colleen."

"Hello, Mrs. Butler."

Elissa shook her head. The crux of all of her problems seemed to be that she was now Mrs. Butler. "Yes, I'm she and all that may entail."

"Is it good to be a rich man's wife? Has he started spoiling you rotten?" Colleen's eagerness was tangible through the phone.

"There has been no spoiling. We did see Joy at church earlier, and Liam did very well." Very well didn't even begin to cover what had happened today.

"We haven't had any time alone, so I need the deets on why you decided to become Mrs. Butler."

"You don't think I was won over by his good looks and personality?" Elissa said sarcastically.

"Spill!"

"Okay, but you have to keep the details quiet and not tell a soul."

"I swear. Tell me!"

Elissa smiled. "You know, you sound really eager for a lawyer."

"If you don't tell me, who else could you tell? I'm good at keeping secrets. I didn't tell when you put fake hair in your head because you had cut that chunk out."

"I can't believe you remember that."

"I didn't tell when you used that new soap and broke out on your whole body and we had to put calamine on you and hide you in my place for a sleepover while my parents were away. I mean I have pictures but I didn't tell a soul!"

"Fine, fine, I'll spill. You know when I started Green Magic?"

"Yeah."

"Well, Aunt Becky loaned me some money. She said she

was going to invest it and it wasn't really important. I used it and I just found out that it was a huge chunk of her retirement funds. She's thinking of going back to work to make back the money if I don't return it."

"Wow. That is a big one to tote around. I'd think that when you told Liam about your plight, he'd have been very supportive. I mean, you're both trying to make the elder matriarchs of your families happy. So what did he say?"

Until Colleen had said it out loud, Elissa had not really thought about it that way.

"You are probably right, Colleen. The problem is that I never told Liam why I needed the money or what I was going to use it for."

"Why not, Elissa?"

"Liam already thinks the worst of me, and I'm going to let him continue to think that. We know there is no hope or future for us beyond our business arrangement. He and I couldn't make our relationship work when we were in college, and we had no responsibilities back then. What would we do now? He's got more money than I've ever seen. Every little step he takes, someone is there to report it or broadcast it. No, he lives a different life than I do. If ever there was a chance of a lasting relationship between us, we missed that boat."

"I just want to throw it out there that I am beyond hurt that you didn't come to me," Colleen said in a low voice.

"First, I know you would give me anything of yours. However, this is my mess. I don't want to go from owing Aunt Becky to owing you. And before you start yelling, I know you wouldn't say I owed it, but I'd feel like I owed it."

Elissa didn't want to shine any other lights on Colleen. If there was a way to discredit her or give her a backhanded compliment, the town found it. If Colleen had given Elissa the money, the teller at the bank would have told her boyfriend that Colleen had moved a big amount. Like hawks they would have waited to see what Colleen spent the money on. If Aunt Becky had mentioned how good a friend Colleen is to try to make her look good that would have fed the rumor mill in the worst way. The bank teller's boyfriend would have told his mother how Colleen had to give Elissa the money for a hush-hush issue. Finally, the mother would have told everyone that their fears were confirmed: Colleen was using her looks for something illicit, and she was paying Elissa to keep quiet. No. Elissa wouldn't go through that with the people of Chusada.

"Well, brainiac, I'm all ears to hear how you are going to give the money back to Aunt Becky without her having a hissy fit."

"That part is the easiest. I'm going to tell my aunt that now I've got the job with the Butler Hotels, I'm going to liquidate Green Magic and give her the money back."

"Uh-huh."

"I need you to be encouraging now," Elissa said.

"I would be if you made any sense. So let me get this straight. Your aunt gave you some money. You tried to make the business work for a year or two. You made practically no money, but you bought supplies and such to keep you going for that time. Now you have decided to walk away, and you can give her back all of the money she gave you. Once she tells that story, you may have people turning up on your doorstep to learn how to run a no-risk business venture."

"All right, all right. You've made your point."

"Now that I've done my duty and made sure my friend is okay, let's get to the really juicy stuff. I know we are not looking at happily ever after, but are you telling me you don't feel a thing being around Liam? I'm your bestie. Come on!"

How should Elissa answer? Her fingers went to an errant strand of hair at her ear. Elissa placed her hand in her lap and then closed her eyes.

"I'm surprised we're talking so much about me. I thought the fireworks were going off between you and Travers."

"You know, I give Travers some leeway, because the man has great height on him! I can forgive a whole lot of a tall man. If only he wasn't a weasel on the wrong side of this arrangement. Please note, I did notice your deflection to the other side. Good job, by the way. I'll leave it alone. I just want to be sure you are not becoming one more victim of the Wild Billionaire of Chusada."

Both of them laughed. When they were done, Elissa felt lighter and better. Colleen was her rock and things would get better. Elissa decided she'd get some fresh air, and before she opened the door, she heard Liam talking.

"Yes, I'm a big fan of reading the Bible. It has it all, including women, war, and death."

Elissa pulled open the door, and three people turned as if surprised to see her: Liam, Joy, and Joy's ten-year-old son, Peter.

"Liam, what are you doing?" Elissa looked horrified.

Liam glanced at Peter, who was now holding his Bible with a new reverence. Joy, who had come to pump Liam for some extra information, had the look of horror, as well. Liam shrugged. *Can't win them all.*

Joy gathered Peter. "We'll be leaving you two, as it seems you both have some talking to do."

Joy hurried away, moving mighty fast for a woman who had just spent the last twenty minutes trying to find out why, when he could have anyone, he would choose to be with Elissa. When he knew they were firmly on their way, he looked back at Elissa.

"You know —"

She held up her hand. "He's a ten-year-old boy. What were you thinking?" she asked through clenched teeth.

"I was thinking I remembered what it was like to be a ten-year-old boy and those three topics were high on my list."

"I was going to come outside and relax. I thought if I saw you, we'd be able to have an intelligent conversation," she said as she walked by him. "I can see I was sooo wrong."

"Is this the way you imagined we'd fix problems? You'd have your say and then you'd walk away?"

Elissa stopped and faced him. He could count on her not running. He wasn't sure what she was about to hit him with, but whatever it was, he preferred that to her just ignoring him—especially when he hadn't been able to get her out of his thoughts since they'd kissed. Had it even been a kiss? He had been kissed before, but Elissa was starting to get under his skin in a welcome kind of way. He had to stop things before they got out of hand. He had to see the differences that would make it impossible for them to do anything else but get a divorce.

"I'm not walking away because we are not having a conversation. You just told a little boy to read the Bible because it has women, war, and death in it?"

"Doesn't it? I mean, it has been a minute since I read it from cover to cover, but I have to say, especially the old testament, it could hold its own when it comes to talking about wars."

She looked up at the sky as if the patience to deal with him would come to her. He could have told her she wasn't alone in seeking that patience. Liam thought about making a joke about how his gran had done that very same move when he was growing up. Elissa might not see the humor in the situation, though.

"Yes, there are those elements in the Bible. However, we'd like to focus on the message," she said, enunciating every word.

He stood up, crossed his arms over his chest, and gave her a lopsided smile. "This has you all worked up, huh?"

Elissa threw her hands in the air and let out a huge sigh. "Again, this is just one more thing you don't seem to understand or are unable to grasp about being here. It's another example of why we need to divorce as soon as possible. Children have fragile minds —"

"Just hold up. I'm not a slow heathen who just fell off the wagon. My gran taught me the Bible."

"Then what happened?!" Elissa pointed in the direction Joy and her son had gone.

"Nothing happened. I told him why he needed to read it and that the message would come with it. I'm pretty sure there isn't a 'Minus Message' version of the Bible."

"Liam, you have to be mindful of what you do."

"Hey, I'm mindful. I know my Bible. I probably know it just as well as you."

She stood with her hands on her hips and a smile breaking out across her face.

"I'm one of the Sunday school teachers. It wouldn't be fair to you if I test you on that."

Liam pushed away from the house and walked until he was a foot in front of her. "I'll take that as being forewarned. I know that when he reads it, he'll find that it's filled with bold, amazing women. My gran taught me that." He saw Elissa stop and wondered what he had said that was so wrong.

"I remember," she whispered.

He started to ask when, but it came to him. She had been there the day his gran had come to the college to tell him his granddad was sick. They didn't know how much time he had, but they were living each day like it was their forever day and their last day.

After Gran left, he had lain in Elissa's arms and let silent tears fall down his face. He'd told her how his grandfather was a hard taskmaster but his idol. Then Liam had told her he thought the strongest person on the planet was his gran. She believed in love even while his granddad was dying, and she'd never once blamed anyone else or changed the way she loved him. Liam wasn't sure he could do that, but his gran was the example of the strength of women.

That night he had told Elissa the strength he had seen in his grandmother, he had seen in her.

"Elissa, I —"

"Shh, Liam. Just leave it alone. We both know why we're in the situation we're in. Let's not complicate it by trying to look for something that's been gone for years."

Liam didn't stop her as she went back into the house. He wasn't one to make the same mistake twice, but he got the feeling he just had.

CHAPTER FIFTEEN

It was a brand new day, and Elissa needed to try two of the new items on her menu. She was going to focus on that and not on her husband. In fact, Elissa wasn't going to concern herself with her spouse at all. She'd forget about the kiss and forget about how he used to look at her years ago in school.

Today, she planned to cook fish. Green Magic usually only did non-meat of any kind, but she wanted a larger appeal and it was on the list of options by the client. As she got out her salmon, she admired how bright the fish was and how pronounced the white lines of fat uniformly spread across the fillet.

Uniformity and control. Those were things her wild billionaire of a husband would know nothing about. Some of the stories had to be true for the title of Wild Billionaire to stick to him, right?

It didn't matter. Liam was a corporate executive who

only looked out for himself. He didn't do anything for anyone unless there was some benefit to him.

Elissa had already cut up garlic, scallions, ginger and salted black beans and put them in a skillet to brown a bit. She had spent a lot of time on this dish; it was nutritionally balanced and easily made in large batches. Elissa just had to make sure it could be made in a certain amount of time and to find out how long its holding time was before it started to lose flavor. She had already done one before, but was starting from scratch with this lovely piece of fish.

"I see I arrived just in the nick of time," Liam murmured.

"Go away. I'm doing Green Magic business."

"Well, then, I should really stay. You're going to be cooking this meal in my hotel, right?"

She put her hands down on the counter on both sides of the fish. For a moment, she considered picking up the fillet and walloping him with it.

"Why don't I finish this, and then we can—"

"No, it's no problem. I won't bother you. I'm just here to watch and see."

"That's the whole notion of bothering me," Elissa murmured.

"Did you say something?"

"No, it's fine. Just stay there. I should be done soon."

"I don't want to be a pain or anything, but I wanted to know if you would be open to some constructive criticism?"

She stopped and had to look up at the ceiling. "On what?"

"I see the other tray of fish. Are you going to make that same thing, only better this time?"

"There's nothing wrong with that other dish, and yes, I'm going to make it again."

"Well, I should tell you not to bother," Liam said matter-of-factly.

"Oh, really? Why and how did you come to this conclusion?" she asked through clenched teeth.

He walked past Elissa, got a bag of chips and began to eat them. "That dish is ugly!"

"It's ugly? Who cares? I'll put some garnish on it later. It's healthy and—"

"I'd rather not be so healthy and eat food I like."

"You don't know if you don't like it, because—"

"Well, no one wants to eat ugly food, so I know I don't like it because I wouldn't eat that!"

As he was popping another chip into his mouth, Elissa faced him. Liam shrugged and then rinsed his hands in the sink.

"Look, I'm sorry, but I'm just saying no one wants to eat ugly food. The fish is pretty, but what is that stuff sprinkled over it? It looks like leftover birdseed cases."

"It's called quinoa. It's healthy, and it's being used in all of the—"

"You could try some salad instead? The color of the salad will really make the fish pop. What do you think of that?"

Elissa studied the dish and saw what he was saying. It was ugly. How could she have missed this? Her shoulders slumped and he cleared his throat.

"Don't beat yourself up. It's my job to give feedback. Not to change the subject, but we need to work on something that will be very important."

Her first reaction was to jump up and say, "What could be more important than this job?" Elissa sighed. "Go ahead."

"Hey, first, don't get put out about the food. It happens.

I look at all sorts of things for the hotel. Now we need to address this issue we have."

Elissa sat down. The fish meal was a no-go. Her mind had already started sifting through recipes to replace it.

"We have to get to know each other, so Gran doesn't suspect a thing."

"We already met with your gran and she was fine."

"Yes, that was then, but I want to make sure we are both prepared, so let's go over some common things," Liam said.

"Okay. What do you want to know?"

"Your favorite color?"

"Red," Elissa said.

"Red. Are you sure?"

"Really? Are you going to say red is an ugly color?"

"It's a great color. I happen to like it myself."

"Oh!"

"You know, red wasn't your favorite color before," Liam said.

These moments were coming more often than not. Would he remember if he didn't care maybe even a little?

"Well, people change. I like red now."

Liam nodded. "Your favorite food used to be candy."

She shook her head. "It's cookies. Chocolate chip, to be precise. And you?"

Liam held up his hand. "Before I respond to that, I'd like you to answer two more questions. Hold on, let me get a piece of paper. I'm going to write down my answers, so you don't forget." Liam scrambled until he found the paper on the table behind him.

"I've got mine written down, so let's go." Liam's smooth voice was like a siren's call.

What was his game? "Okay. Go for it."

"Your favorite flower and your favorite place to go on a date."

"A rose and a museum," Elissa said triumphantly.

"Are you sure?" Liam asked.

"Yes, I am. I know they're not what they were before, but this is a good way to check where our interests are now that we're grown up."

Liam stood and leaned in close.

Elissa froze. Her heart jumped and her pulse ticked up a notch. Certainly he would be able to hear it. If she played it cool maybe, at this point she didn't even know what she wanted to happen now. "Liam? What is it?"

"I'm leaving now and after I go, you can look at my paper. I don't think we'll have any problems pretending to be compatible." His breath brushed her ear and he walked out of the kitchen.

Elissa waited until she'd heard the door close before grabbing the paper and opening it. Two words were written in Liam's blocked, all caps writing.

Rose. Museum.

CHAPTER SIXTEEN

"Is this some sort of payback from yesterday?" Liam moaned as he got into the car.

"No, this is the result of someone making plans with his grandmother and then telling her any time that worked for her would work for us."

"She's retired. She doesn't have to work. I thought we were safe!"

"She's retired, yes, not incapacitated. Your gran still does a lot of work for this town. You work in New York City, only coming home on holidays, but your gran lives here and is a big part of this town. There have been some lean years for some families here. To the town, the Butler name has always been associated with helping out."

Liam waved his hand in the air and reclined the seat. "I can't hear about the goodness of my family yet. I haven't had any coffee. Please tell me we can stop by a café and get a large coffee."

"I'm not sure how you've managed to survive this long. Coffee is so bad for you. It kicks your nerves up and it makes you jittery. Your staff is probably on pins and needles when you get a cup of coffee."

"My staff is competing to bring me the coffee first. Whoever can get it before I do, is pretty much guaranteed a raise!"

Elissa sniffed as she drove. "If it's any consolation, I'm told your gran has the same reverence for coffee that you do, so I'm sure she will have some for you when we get there. She gets together with Aunt Becky because they are both on the church board. So I know they've exchanged coffees and teas in the past."

"You're my wife now, Elissa. It had to be in one of our vows that you would make sure I had coffee all the days of my life, and to your observation, yes, I am aware of my gran's love of coffee."

Elissa smiled. "No, I promised to love and honor you, whatever that may mean to me. You promised I could have access to your money, also known as your health and well-being."

Liam lifted his head from the seat. "I didn't do that!"

"Oh, you did. I was a bit surprised, but I know when you are in the moment, these things can get by you."

Liam grunted and flopped back down in his seat. "Give me coffee and I won't tell that you used your womanly wiles on me to get that agreement."

Elissa laughed. "I hate to be the one to remind you, but the reason you are in this 'mess,' as you call it, is because of the woman we are on our way to see."

"I'm weak now, Elissa. Don't throw a man's shortcomings at him when he's down."

"Actually, I think it's kind of cute. You are going through all of this for your grandmother."

Cute. Oh, yes, this day was turning into a new experience. Liam couldn't even imagine what would happen if Travers heard Elissa calling him cute. Liam liked to think he was a beast in the boardroom and a terror during negotiations. Cute? Not so much. But, Elissa was right about his relationship with Gran. He couldn't think of a single thing his grandmother could ask him that he would say no to. She'd been there for him always. Gran didn't always agree with him, but she still supported his decisions, which was one of the reasons he'd been so shocked to hear she'd been working against him with the board. He would find out who was doing the work on the board members, and he'd probably discover that someone was manipulating and taking advantage of his gran.

Liam had to remember that no matter what kind words came out of Elissa's mouth, she was in the money game, as well. If not for the cash, she wouldn't be here at all. Was she still holding a grudge from college? He couldn't tell; he just didn't get women as a whole. This year, having dealt with woman after woman trying to trick him into a relationship, he should be grateful that the one he had with Elissa was at least honest in its selfish ends.

Nope, Elissa was just like all the rest of those women. The only difference: she had fessed up to it. At least they had that much honesty between them. He closed his eyes and let the rocking of the car take him away from a truth that wasn't so comforting.

How did the man fall asleep so quickly?

They were at his grandmother's and Elissa had tapped

Liam on the shoulder twice. He hadn't budged. No worries. Elissa looked at her watch and saw they had ten minutes before they were supposed to be at the door. She could let him sleep, but at this rate, she wasn't in favor of the idea. She had an idea.

Elissa got out of the car and opened Liam's door. She took his feet out and put them on the ground. His legs were muscular and heavy in his blue jeans. She didn't even want to think about how his legs would look in the summer in a nice pair of khaki shorts.

Focus, Elissa.

She stood back and kicked his foot. Liam groaned but didn't budge.

"Oh, come on!" She leaned in the car and whispered, "Liam, stock is down."

"Liam, I see reporters."

Neither statement stirred him. Just when Elissa thought she was going to have to get some water, she let out a breath and muttered, "Had I known you'd be like this, I'd have brought you coffee."

"Coffee!"

Liam jerked forward and his forehead hit hers. Elissa instinctively reached for her head, but when Liam had collided with her, he'd kept going forward. She stumbled and Liam tumbled out of the car and brought both of them down to the pavement.

At the same moment, Elissa heard the door to the house open.

"Liam!" she called.

"Coffee?" Liam slurred.

"I saw you drive up, then the next thing I know your both lying on the pavement, so I thought I better come out to make sure you two are okay," Liam's grandmother said with a questioning look. "I can see the honeymoon is still going on. Come in when you're ready. I'm in the kitchen."

As his grandmother was walking away, Liam opened both eyes.

"Gran?"

"You big clumsy oaf! Get off of me. I can't believe your gran saw us like this."

Liam looked down. "You are not coffee."

Elissa closed her eyes and tried to find her center, so she didn't scream like a banshee. "I am not coffee and you are not light, so if you please?"

As if he became aware of where he was and with whom, he rolled away from Elissa.

"I'm sorry," he murmured.

Elissa brushed herself off and then sighed. "Yeah, I think there will be a lot of apologizing before the day is over. Let's go, and I'll definitely make sure you have your coffee from now on."

Elissa had stepped away from the table. As Liam had anticipated, his grandmother began the interrogation.

"Are you well, Liam, and is everything ok with Elissa?"

He couldn't stand to see his gran worried.

"I'm well. Elissa and I are good."

Gran smiled and then nodded. "Well, today we need to go into town. I visit a couple of places every week, and I want to make sure everyone knows you're married. I also want it to be known we've extended our family."

"Is there a problem?"

"No problem, Liam. Just the way things are done in small towns."

"I don't know how you stay here."

His grandmother smiled. "I stay here because this is where I spent most of my time with your grandfather. When I'm feeling down, I can find comfort in things and places. Living in a big city is wonderful, but it doesn't have your granddad's spirit."

"I didn't know you were doing the whole town thing."

His grandmother waved him off.

"Butlers have always done the 'town thing.' Most of the time when we were doing it, you were in New York, running the hotels. It will be good for you to know the people who know your wife and where you both live."

Liam smiled. "No worries. I've got that."

Elissa returned when he and Gran were laughing. His wife smiled at them both, and when he didn't drop his gaze, she glanced away with a smile. He could get used to this. He could get used to her. If only he could trust her.

When she looked back up at him with a timid smile, he turned away. What was he doing? He'd chosen Elissa because she was the last woman he wanted to be with. He just had to remember that.

She shouldn't be here with him and his gran in this close moment. Elissa had made it clear she'd married Liam for his money. What made him so angry was how inconsistent her greed seemed to be with what he sensed in her. He did a lot of his work by his instincts, and right now, his instincts were telling him a different tale than what he'd gotten from her.

Liam disliked things that didn't add up. He couldn't really deal with the anomaly now while he was fighting for his company. They all got into the car and drove to town, but Liam's thoughts weighed on his mind and didn't let him enjoy the view or allow him to be able to talk to his gran in the car. When they parked and everyone exited, his gran touched his shoulder.

"Are you all right, Liam?"

"Yes. I'm sorry, I'm distracted."

"Well, perk up. I have an announcement."

Elissa looked over the top of the car and Gran smiled. Liam had a horrible feeling in his gut, but to please his grandmother, he'd deal.

"Elissa, come here, dear."

When the both of them were in front of Gran, she said, "I've got a surprise for you. I'm going to throw you a wedding!"

Liam and Elissa glanced at one another. Then Liam straightened up.

"Gran, we're already—"

"Psshaw! You need to have your marriage witnessed by everyone. I wasn't sure about your relationship, but after this morning and what I heard about you two at the picnic grounds, I'm sure. It'll be a replica of my wedding to your granddad, Liam. I've started the arrangements already! I've been dying to tell you both!"

Liam looked again at Elissa, who was tucking her hair behind her ear.

"What do you think, Elissa?" Gran asked.

"I think it's the kindest thing anyone has ever done, and you've gone above and beyond," Elissa responded.

Liam wanted to kick himself. If he had been more focused on Gran and not so much on Elissa and whatever her true nature might be, he would have seen this coming. When his grandmother turned to him, he hoped his smile looked genuine and not phony.

Gran cupped his chin. "Your granddad would be so proud of you now. We both wanted to make sure that you didn't marry the company and forget about yourself. He saw a lot of people do that in the hotel industry. One of the reasons he chose the hotel business was because it was something he enjoyed doing all the time. He never tired of it, but he could leave it and have a life.

"At any rate, I won't bore you with details. What I want is to celebrate your good fortune. And so I can introduce my new granddaughter- in- law." Gran faced his wife, whose posture had stiffened. Liam was surprised Gran didn't tap Elissa to make sure she could still move.

"You know, my dear, I always liked you. Even when Liam was in college, you were a good woman who could stand up to him."

Liam cleared his throat. "Well, I guess some things come back to where they started." Trying to move past this train of thought, he said, "Let's get the items done for the day."

Gran laughed. "Fine. I won't embarrass you now, but you have to let me brag a little bit." She pointed down the street. "We can start by going to the bakery. I like to go there for a little something sweet."

"Do you now?" Liam smiled.

"Don't judge. I need some little pleasures in my life."

"Why don't you two go ahead? I'll catch up," Elissa said.

"No problem, dear. If we aren't at the bakery, we'll be at the café," Gran said.

Elissa nodded and walked off. He watched her for a moment. When she passed most of the stores on the block, his anger flared. She headed in the direction of the bank.

Gran tapped him on the shoulder.

"Now, now. Whatever you're thinking, get rid of it. You two have been married for less than a week. Whatever has you looking at her that way, you can work out. You'll see."

"Ever the optimist, Gran."

"No, Liam, I know both of your temperaments. I'm a realist first and a romantic second. You should remember that. Anyway, let's go and get me a bear claw," she said with a grin.

"Sure." The bank wasn't the only place in the direction Elissa was going, but he'd bet she couldn't wait to check if he had sent the money.

CHAPTER SEVENTEEN

Gran pushed open the door, and the smell of baked goods and sweets wafted out and wrapped themselves around Liam. Liam smiled as his gran made sure to get to the door before him.

"You see? The smell alone is worth it."

At the counter, two younger women were standing taller and smiling so wide, he was sure they would hurt their faces. When the door closed, an older woman came from the rear of the bakery. She wore a plastic cap on her head and her white apron said 'Baker or Butcher. You Decide.'

"Clara Butler. I'm so glad you came in today."

"I hadn't expected to, Sasha, but I'm in town with my grandson and his new wife," Gran said.

Sasha looked over her shoulder at the girls behind the counter.

"Hey, the both of you. To the back. He's spoken for already!"

Sasha turned back to Liam and his grandmother.

"Ah, yes. I'd heard the hometown boy who's done well had married the health nut chef. Quite a union."

Liam offered his hand. "I'm actually the town billionaire, not that I count that stuff anymore. But yes, I'm the hometown boy who did well and who married an innovative woman."

Sasha took a step back and studied Liam with slitted eyes.

"Wait, wait, I do recall seeing you on television a couple days or maybe a week ago. You were on the news in a robe. I guess the suddenness of the marriage after a scene like that shouldn't take anyone by surprise."

The only sound in the room was the slight gasp from one of the two girls who had not made it into the back of the shop yet.

"Now that I see him in person, I can understand why she may have married him right away—no matter what it would look like after they were married."

All of a sudden, the importance of maintaining a person's reputation in this town became very clear to Liam. He hadn't really given enough thought to what Elissa was in for. He couldn't stand gossip or people being in his business all the time. Now here he was trying to save his company, and Elissa was putting her reputation on the line.

"My, my, my, Sasha. That wasn't charitable of you at all," Gran said sweetly.

Liam had instinctively wrapped his arm around his grandmother. Now that he heard that voice coming out of her—so smooth and slick, but like she was the one who had the power—he wasn't so keen on touching her.

"You are the last person who should talk about quick changes," Gran said. "Today your shop is the town bakery, but not long ago, it was a drive-thru 7-Eleven. Before that, a massage parlor. Yes, everyone can tell you are definitely the queen of making changes on the fly."

Sasha held up her hands and shook her head at the same time.

"No, no. I'm not saying moving quickly is bad," Sasha protested.

"Good. I'm glad you're not criticizing my new granddaughter-in-law. But just to make sure we get off on the right foot, I think it's appropriate for you to apologize to Liam."

"Of course, of course. Please excuse me, Liam. It's already been a long day."

Gran smiled and nodded. She went up and down the aisles where open racks filled with fresh pastries were lined on baking sheets with tongs and little plastic bags next to them. Every so often, she would reach her hand out as if to grab a pastry. Then she would shake her head and continue her perusing. After about fifteen minutes, and with her most gracious smile, Gran said, "It turns out I've lost my taste for sweets today. Thank you, Sasha." His grandmother exited like the queen she was.

When they left the air-conditioned bakery, the Florida heat welcomed them with a warm breeze that offered little comfort. Liam wasn't sure he could have even said if it was hot or cold out. His grandfather had always said his grandmother had a kind heart and defended those she loved, but until today, Liam had never seen it. On top of never seeing it, it had never been for him.

She'd always talked of responsibility, how Liam must take the lead, and how Liam had to be the one to follow in his grandfather's footsteps. Liam needed to become all of the men that his father hadn't been able to. When Liam thought about his childhood, he remembered how his grandmother would pat him on the back and tell him how lucky he was to be walking in his granddad's footsteps. But today, Liam's grandmother had stood up for him just the way he was.

Gran talked about what they would do once they hit the café. Apparently, she made monthly visits to cafés and libraries to speak to the local people and understand what their concerns were. She wasn't an elected official or the mayor, but she had enough input on the board that people listened to her.

"Since there were no snacks to be had at the bakery, I guess we're going to have to get a bite to eat at the café. Are you hungry , Liam?"

"I'm sorry. What were you saying?"

"Dear boy, Elissa hasn't been gone that long. I need you to focus so that we can get through the next half hour with the town."

Liam looked in the direction Elissa had gone. "Don't you think we should go and pick up Elissa first? That way, we can all get seated at the same time."

"No, we don't want to bother her. I'm sure she has a few quick errands to run that don't include us." Gran patted him on the shoulder. "You don't have to worry about her. She's in town with her own people. This isn't New York and she'll be just fine."

Finally, Liam understood what his Gran was saying. "You think I'm concerned about Elissa's safety?"

Gran patted him on the shoulder again and shook her head. "It's okay. We won't talk about it. I will tell you this is just one of those things you're going to have to learn to deal with. You can't always be together at the hip."

Liam muttered under his breath. No, Elissa probably wanted to be connected at the wallet.

CHAPTER EIGHTEEN

Historically speaking, the bank had once been the old school. All of the classrooms had been converted into conference rooms. The rest of the first floor had been opened up and tellers lined the floor.

Customers had to walk through the bank and go all the way to the back to find the investment banker's office, which actually used to be the old janitorial office. The room had only one desk, because there was only one investment banker, named Fred Landers, on site. Elissa knew Fred. They had gone to school together. Back then, Fred had always been picked on and bullied. She'd felt sorry for him, but something about him just always seemed to be a little off.

It probably wasn't until the incident at the church that she really had her suspicions about Fred. While he was a nice enough guy, she just didn't think he was a trustworthy one. At the end of the day, Fred still wanted to be accepted, and he'd do whatever he had to in order to get that acceptance.

Elissa waited patiently for him to return to his office. When Fred finally made it back in, she could tell he had gained a few pounds since she'd last seen him. When he sat down, the chair creaked and rocked back and forth.

"Hello, Ms. Dane. How can I help you?"

Elissa smiled. "Actually, I'm not here to get any help for myself, I just need to clear up an account."

"I know all of my accounts. You don't have one set up with me, Elissa. Maybe you have me confused with someone else here at the bank?"

"I'm in the right place."

"I heard some rumblings in town that you were going to get married."

"I'm not a Dane any longer. Recently, I became Mrs. Liam Butler."

"Well, that's a good coup for you and your family."

The first feeling that something wasn't quite right started to sneak up Elissa's back. Fred's smile was too wide, and all of his responses were just too friendly.

"What can I do for you today, and whose account are we talking about?" Fred asked with a bit of a bite in his voice.

Elissa knew she should have let it go but she couldn't.

"I'm sorry. It must be a good coup for my family and me?" Elissa asked.

Fred held up his hands. "Sorry. I didn't mean it in any kind of negative way. You know how small towns are. Everybody remembers things. Not that long ago, your aunt had that little run-in with the church treasury. So getting married to the town's richest bachelor has got to be a coup for you, as well as her. Now that you have the Butler name, you won't have to worry about those little things being brought up anymore."

Elissa put on a fake smile. She needed to get out of this office as soon as possible before she did something to the Pillsbury Doughboy sitting across from her. "That's all in the past now, and I'm here to discuss a new future. Besides, that incident with the treasury is old news."

"A new future? Are you saying that you are expecting?" Fred snickered. "Well, that would explain why you got married so quickly."

If Elissa had to keep the smile on her face any longer, it would crack and she would lash out.

"No, Fred, I'm not in the family way. I'd like to discuss Aunt Becky's retirement account." Elissa held out the check for $80,000 and slid it across the desk.

Fred looked at it, picked it up and then held the check up to the light. Then he ran his thumbs over it, as if seeing whether the ink would smudge. "Is this check any good?"

"It is. You can verify it now. I borrowed this amount from Aunt Becky, and she took out a loan from her retirement fund. I'd like to pay back that loan in full now."

Fred sat back in his chair. His oily smile returned, he placed the check on his desk and then he folded his pudgy little fingers together. "I appreciate you trying to help out your aunt, Elissa, but I'm afraid this just won't do. Have you told her about this? I don't think she would take kindly to you trying to settle her debt."

"Fred, while I appreciate your concern, I really don't think it's any of your business how I settle this with Aunt Becky."

The man had started turning red around the collar. With

his finger, he kept trying to pull his collar away from his fat neck, but it wasn't helping.

"Do you have any other questions, Fred? Check with the bank now if you'd like to confirm the funds. I don't have a problem with that or waiting."

"That's not going to be necessary. When I explain things to you, you'll understand there's a much deeper and graver problem."

A cold knot of fear settled in Elissa's stomach. She folded her hands in her lap and waited. Whatever was wrong, it was enough to get the Pillsbury Doughboy all worked up. So here she sat in his office with the door closed waiting to find out what was Fred's game.

"I'm afraid I'm not going to be able to accept the money on behalf of your aunt," Fred said, looking sad.

"What do you mean? Why can't you accept the money?"

"Well, you see, all of the cash was taken out of the retirement fund your Aunt Becky was part of. So she could go ahead and put the money back in, and of course, I could go and invest it. However, it's going to look like she went ahead and took her money out and then suddenly all the rest of the cash is stolen. Then once all the funds were gone, and it was safe again, she puts her money back in."

It had finally happened. Fred had been in this small town for so long, he'd finally lost his grasp on reality. Fred had embezzled all of the money out of the retirement fund and he was trying to put the blame on Aunt Becky. She needed some clarity on what had already been done but she wasn't going to find that out now from Mr. Dishonest.

Fred spread his hands wide, as if he intended to offer her

something. "You have to see how this all works out, Elissa. I was never getting anywhere in this town. But this retirement fund had ten people who really put in a lot of cash. The rest of the folks in the fund didn't have more than a couple of thousand, but some, like your aunt, had money. When she asked me for that loan, it was the best thing ever. I had a plan, and I knew it was going to work."

Elissa shook her head and stood up. "I don't know anything about your plan, and I really don't care to know. What I can tell you is, I'm giving you the money to pay off that loan for my aunt. You need to find out on your own what happened to the rest of the money. I can't believe you would steal from people you've known all of your life."

"Are you really going to get on that soapbox now? You know everyone is going to believe that your aunt had something to do with the missing money. She had that incident with the treasury at the church, which was never resolved. We just all agreed to look the other way, because it was such a small amount. By the time I finish talking about it, everyone in town will understand the treasury was just her practice run before she stole the money from the retirement fund."

"That's the dumbest plan, Fred. No one will believe Aunt Becky stole the money. There's no way she even could have done it."

"See, when you say it that way, it doesn't sound believable. But when people hear how she was struggling financially, that she planned to go back to work, then they'll understand she was just taking little dribs and drabs of money, and then all of a sudden, it was gone. I mean, we just have to look at the bank records to see that's been happening."

"What bank records? My aunt didn't do a thing!"

"Maybe she did, and maybe she didn't, but you have to ask yourself some questions. One: Do you want me to start these rumors in Chusada? With this scandal, she'll be ostracized. That would be a shame. Two: How would your new husband like to find out he's married to the niece of an embezzler? He might not care, seeing how fast you got him to the altar, but his board might. Right now, I don't think he can take that scandal."

"What do you want?"

"The same thing everybody wants: the money."

"What do you want me to do, Fred?"

"I'm willing to be reasonable with you, Elissa. The only thing you must do is keep your money. In a couple of weeks, a story will break about how someone sifted funds out of the account. There'll be no mention of Aunt Becky. You have the cash, so you can go ahead and put it someplace else."

Elissa wanted to jump across the desk and humble the Pillsbury Doughboy, who sat looking smug. Instead, she had to think. She couldn't even imagine going to Liam right now to explain, when he was fighting to keep his position with the board.

"Fred, put ALL the money back!"

"Put the money back," Fred mocked. "That comes straight from the mouth of someone who has never needed money or been without. No, I will not put that money back. I earned it. This town bullied me, and all of you let it happen. Even though I went away and got a degree, where did you all place me? In the janitorial hole. No, I will not give the money back. It's mine. I suggest you go back home, or wherever it is that you were going, and you think on the idea that you need to do what's right for everybody. Right for you, right for your aunt, and right for Liam, your brand-new, rich husband."

Elissa shielded her eyes as she walked out of the bank. It figured that the snake would be in the coldest part of the building. What was she going to do?

Think, Elissa. What are your options? Option A was to take the Pillsbury Doughboy out and overfeed him until he had a heart attack. Option B was to offer him more cash, and she could just see how that would go. How could she explain to Liam she needed more money? There was always option C but the way the town was, everyone would know about the whole incident and that wouldn't save Aunt Becky's reputation at all.

Okay, a lot of things were going to happen, but she was not going to pay off Fred. But he had a point: Aunt Becky lived in this town and breathed in this town. She was a working member of the church, and if she became caught up in a scandal, everybody would be polite to her in the street, but she'd never be a part of the community again. Aunt Becky would lose the life she had worked so hard to build and keep.

Elissa had walked over to the bakery. When she went in the door, she saw Sasha talking to Joy. Just what she did not need in her life right now. Elissa thought about backing out of the shop, but just then, Joy turned and spotted her.

"Hello, Elissa. After that touching scene in front of the church, I'm surprised to see you without your husband. I mean, you still do have a husband, don't you?" Joy asked.

"Hello, Joy. Yes, my husband and I are fine. Thank you for asking. I just came in to see if they were still here, as we all came into town together today."

Elissa really couldn't take anything else. She just wanted to find Liam and his grandmother and go home.

"As involved as your husband is with his work in the city, I'm just wondering if that's going to take a toll on you and your aunt? I know Becky does a lot of work in the church. That may all change as soon as you and Liam decide to have children, of course."

Elissa was beyond frustrated. Joy was talking about her taking Aunt Becky away from everything that she knew. Elissa felt the blood pumping through her veins and she had to flex her hands so she wouldn't reach for her by the hair. Oh how she wanted to act like a five year old and tell Joy, 'let's settle this in the yard!'

"Thank you for your concern, Joy, but I wouldn't worry about it. Aunt Becky loves being here."

"So, are you saying there are no children on the way?"

"Why is everybody so concerned about what is going on in my uterus? Let me be clear, Joy. I did not rush to get married because I was pregnant. Liam and I experienced deep, moving feelings that made us both know we were the one, so we got married." Elissa tucked a strand of hair behind her ear and then folded her arms. "Now, if you will excuse me. Thank you."

Sasha came up to her with a bag in her hand.

"Elissa, please give this bear claw to Clara for me. When they came in, we were not on good speaking terms, but I want no hard feelings. Will you please do me this favor?"

"Of course." They weren't on good speaking terms? Sasha and Clara were almost besties because Clara came into the bakery at least once a week. What else could have gone wrong? Elissa needed to find Liam and his gran; they would probably be at the café getting a quick bite to eat, which Elissa would love right now. She left the bakery, walked the two blocks down to the café, and found a long line. All of the people stood holding papers. Finally, Elissa had to ask.

"Excuse me, but why are you all standing in this line?"

"The Butlers are in. Today, Clara Butler has decided to celebrate her grandson getting married by listening to what people need and paying off some of their bills. You might get your bill paid, or you might even get a job at one of the Butler Hotels. They just told a couple of folks, but I guess word spread, and now people are hurrying to get in the line."

Elissa walked by the line, and a couple of folks gave her dirty looks. When she got to the front of the café and opened the door, a waitress immediately came to her. "What are you here for? Do you want to have a booth? Are you here for the Butlers?"

"I'm not here for the Butlers. I am a Butler. Could you please take me to them?"

The flustered waitress gave Elissa a second look and then nodded.

"Come this way. Maybe if there's another one of you, we can get this line done so we can get the rest of our restaurant back."

CHAPTER NINETEEN

Elissa walked behind the waitress, who took her directly to her new family. Elissa didn't interrupt the person Liam was talking to; instead, she just listened.

"I'm going to go ahead and pay this bill off, but I want you to take this number and call this man on the card. Tell him Liam sent you. He'll help you make a budget and get your finances in order. That way, you and your daughter will be safe even on one income."

"Are you sure he'll be able to do anything for us with so little coming in? I mean, I don't have a bunch of money to pay an advisor."

"Just tell him I told you to see him. He can call me about the details, okay? You finish your classes and stay in school. You need to do it for you and your daughter."

"Thank you so much, Mr. Butler. Thank you so, so much."

The waitress bumped into Elissa from behind and broke

her concentration. Who was this Mr. Butler? How could he be the same man who'd looked at her as if she was the lowest of the low when she'd taken money from him?

Elissa turned toward the waitress.

"How long have they been sitting here?"

The older woman just laughed. "I've known the Butlers for a long time. Clara comes in here regularly to eat, you know. Now that her grandson is finally married, I knew she'd want to do something but I didn't expect this. I want to say they've been in here maybe half an hour, but if need be, they'll stay until all the people are done."

Elissa pulled up a seat next to the table and scooted closer to Liam. Their thighs were touching underneath the table. And at that moment, when he looked up, they were just themselves without the past between them or the money he'd paid her. If only this could be every day.

Liam smiled. His smile was free of all of the earlier division and judgment. This was the Liam she knew. They had been apart for so long, broken up over something silly, and then they'd been brought back together. Now there was only distrust between them. So many decisions needed to be made. So many people would be affected if she made the wrong choices.

Gazing into Liam's eyes, she remembered. Once upon a time, she had believed in love. She had believed in happily-ever-afters, and she had believed in a white knight named Liam. Small towns had rules. She couldn't go ahead and do something that would reflect badly on Aunt Becky. Having her aunt face criticism for Elissa's foolishness with Liam was a risk she wasn't willing to take. Everyone blamed her aunt for Elissa putting herself out there and waiting for Liam during college. When he didn't show to pick her up, the town murmured that her aunt Becky hadn't raised her right or taught her good judgment. Liam had never understood the town pressures because he was gone most of the time.

She pulled her thigh back and scooted over. Liam stood up and put his hand on Clara's shoulder; he called the older waitress over.

"Please go and collect the names of the folks who are already in line. After that, we won't be adding anymore people. We're leaving now. But let the folks in line know we will call them and they will be able to talk to us then. Okay?"

"No problem," the waitress said.

Clara looked up at Liam. "Are you ready to leave now?"

He bent down and kissed his grandmother on her forehead. "Let's go home. I think you've spread enough joy and goodwill today."

"Nowhere near what I'm really feeling inside." Gran looked between Liam and Elissa and then nodded. "But if you want to, we can certainly go home."

As they left the café, Elissa saw Joy making her way to the front of the line. Joy started arguing with the older waitress who was telling her that her name couldn't be put on the list. Joy looked at Elissa's family as they got into the car and then scoffed and stomped into the café.

When they were all settled in the car, Elissa gave the bear claw to Clara, who smiled and said she would go and see Sasha tomorrow. Elissa took a deep breath and then turned on the car. Liam reached over and touched her hand on the steering wheel.

"Are you okay? Did you get all of your business taken care of?"

This would be her opportunity to tell him and Clara what

was going on. But Elissa's tongue was stilled by the need to protect her aunt.

"I've got some things I still need to work through, but it was definitely informative."

Liam nodded, sat back and closed his eyes as she got ready to drive off. Yes, it had been informative. She'd discovered a man doing retirement fraud in a small town and had to protect her aunt from the embezzler who was nothing more than a fat kid who wanted to get back at everyone in the town.

Liam had brought a desk into the house. Most days, Elissa could hear him talking on the phone and running his business from there. His voice had a deep timbre that lulled her and made her walk a little closer to the door, so she could hear more of it. Here she was sneaking around in her own house just to listen to the sound of her husband's voice. When did the tables turn? Liam was turning out to be everything she had imagined and more. Her days were filled by being with Liam, walking around town, and Liam introducing himself to everyone talking to his grandmother. There were even nights when they were sitting around talking with her aunt that everything seemed perfect.

Then Elissa would go back to her room and see the $80,000 check that hadn't been deposited. Her conversation with Fred would come back to haunt her, and every day, she turned on the news to see if he had gone ahead and spilled the beans. She still hadn't worked out how she was going to fix the situation.

In the meantime, Liam was ingratiating himself with Aunt Becky. He helped her around the house and also helped her find handymen to do work on the home. Liam had called some of his staff at the hotel to fix most issues. Aunt Becky always asked if he could do it. He always said he had someone on the payroll who could.

One night, as Elissa was getting her nightly fix listening to Liam's voice, she sneezed.

"Elissa?"

"Oh, yes, it's me. I was just coming to ask if you wanted some tea or coffee. I know you're working."

"I have to say something to you, Elissa."

"Okay."

"I need to go back to New York." The words hit her like a gut punch. She'd known that playing house in a little town wouldn't work for him for very long. Knowing it and then having to live with it were two different things.

"Let me know when you're going to leave and when you're planning on coming back, and we can plan some other outings." Elissa hoped her voice didn't sound as pathetic and hopeless as she was feeling.

"No, I don't think you understand. We need to go to New York."

In seconds, Elissa felt like a weed that had been drooping and was on its last leg but then perked up in the sun.

"Oh." They needed to go to New York. She was going to be with her husband in the Big Apple.

"How does that sound to you, Elissa?"

She pushed a strand of hair behind her ear. "I think I can make it."

"Do you want to try that again?" Liam said with a

deep laugh. Elissa realized he was watching for her tell.

"I'm good. Really, we can go. I'm sure it's going to be a huge adventure." Elissa folded her hands in front of her to make sure she didn't accidentally touch the strand behind her ear.

"It'll be a huge adventure, I think, since we're about to go meet the board."

"Meet the board? Do you really want me to go? I mean, I don't know anything about meeting people on boards. I can interview for a job no problem, but this board thing… They have so much power. I don't want to do anything to mess up your chances, Liam."

"Are you saying you just don't want to be seen in public with me?"

Elissa looked at a smirking Liam. Going to New York would be great if she was going to get her job. But going to the big city now seemed like the worst idea ever. What would happen if Fred broke the story while she was gone? She couldn't tell Liam about Fred yet.

"If you're comfortable, Liam, then yes, we can both go to see the board."

"Okay, then. What's the problem?"

"I need us to wait until Monday."

"Because on Monday…?"

"I'm catering a child's birthday party. Then we can leave."

"Oh, you have work. No problem. I'll let Travers know that we have to leave after that."

"You don't mind waiting?"

Liam shrugged. "It's work. It's okay. Remember, I've already tasted your food. I know it's good, so I don't mind letting the kids have the experience and something healthy, too. I've got some last-minute reports to do. After that, I'm going to bed, but thanks, I've been meaning to ask you about the trip and everything else has been happening. Thanks, Elissa, for making this easy."

Elissa just nodded and gave a wan smile. She was indeed in too deep. When Liam left this time after their arrangement was over, she didn't think there'd be a way to recover.

CHAPTER TWENTY

Elissa drove him crazy. She was loyal and faithful to her friends and family. She obviously loved her Aunt Becky. Gran loved her already. Elissa seemed to do everything perfectly. The problem was, the caring, sweet, and nurturing woman he saw didn't line up with the opportunistic person who'd taken his check.

He needed to figure her out sooner rather than later. His head was going in one direction, while his heart went back to fond memories of her. Every day the fight continued within himself about who the real Elissa was.

With any other person, he would have told them just to go ahead and ask her already. This hemming and hawing and thinking wasn't getting him anywhere. He had already given her the opportunity to ask him for more money. She hadn't taken it. So what was the big hold up? Why didn't she just come straight out and ask?

The only answer was unattractive: Elissa was looking ahead to their divorce and getting her share of his wealth.

Liam had looked at the rollout plan for the last hour. If he couldn't get his mind off of her, he wasn't going to be able to do any work. Just when he had decided to go and talk to her, his phone rang.

"Hey, Travers."

"Liam. So, did you talk to Elissa about meeting the board?"

"I did. We are good to go. But we're going to have to wait till after Monday."

"Do I dare ask why we have to wait until then?"

Liam cleared his throat and sat up straighter in his chair. "She has a catering event to do."

"She's got work to do that's more important than meeting the board?" Liam heard the hint of laughter in Travers's voice.

"Well, just so you know, it's a little kid's party, and she wants to make sure she keeps her word, so yes, it's important, and we're going to do the party before we come."

A moment of silence passed before Travers started laughing.

"Oh, I have to tell you, Liam, ever since the alleyway, you have just been coming up with the hits. I couldn't have given a better answer in a million years."

"It's not that big of a deal. You know I want to make sure that Elissa can still work, being able to help her save Green Magic was part of the deal."

"Yeah, yeah, what you said. I'll go ahead and get things set up, and I'll let the board know that you value children and that's why we may be late. It's great. I'm surprised I didn't come up with it. Good job, Liam."

"Travers, we're going to have to talk."

"Talk."

"Not everything I say is up for grabs for you to spin to the board or the public."

"Liam?"

"There are folks here who don't want their information out there."

"Liam, we are still focused on the goal, though, right? The goal is to make sure that the board knows you are stable. You can't be stable unless we show them you hang out with families and other people."

"I hear you, and I'm not saying we can't do it, Travers. I'm just saying that I'd like the publicity to be vetted by me first."

"Okay. I think we'll be missing out on great opportunities, but we'll do it your way, Liam."

"Thanks, Travers, for standing by me."

"Of course. The good news is that being in that town has really helped your image. It was a good decision, even though I know you weren't sold on it. How are you, is everything going well for you?"

"It's going. Let's just say people aren't who I thought they were," Liam said, still trying to figure out Elissa.

"Liam, remember the end goal. You're not there to make a go of things. Women haven't been figured out. You're there to make sure you keep your company."

Liam let out a sigh and looked around the room. "I'm working on it, Travers. I'm working on it."

"You had me worried there, man. Well, what about Colleen?"

"Colleen?"

"Yeah, you know, the tall drink of cool water with the

brain. I'll bet she's missing me in that town already. Who else could she go around and spar with?"

"Is that interest I hear in the voice of I'll-always-remain-single Travers? You sure know how to pick them if you are interested in Colleen."

"Don't knock it. There must be something in the water in Chusada. Maybe they raise the women a little differently there. Once you get a taste of them, you have to come back for more."

"You're playing with fire when you're playing with Colleen. That's just my friendly warning to you," Liam said, not entirely understanding what Travers saw in Elissa's bossy friend.

"From the sounds of it, Liam, I'd rather be playing with fire than overthinking things."

The conversation went on for another ten to fifteen minutes, but at the end of it, Liam was thinking about what Travers had said. Liam kept going over and over in his mind what was between him and Elissa. It was time to put all of the questions he had to rest. He got up and walked out of his small makeshift office. The house was compact, and just down the hall was Elissa's bedroom; the door was already cracked open. He knocked on it, and at first, he didn't hear anything. Then when he knocked again, he heard Elissa say, "Yes?"

He pushed open the door. Whatever thought he'd had quickly left him. Elissa stood in the middle of the room. Her hair, still wet, was down, and she was pulling it up into a knot. She had on a green and white dress that fell to mid-calf. She also wore a pair of green flip flops, and they had large flowers on top. He couldn't remember a woman who'd looked more beautiful.

With her arms held high and holding her hair on top of

her head, he could see the errant curls she was trying to get under control. A couple strands of her hair had found a way to escape and molded to her face from her temple to her chin. She was innocence and temptation, all wrapped up in one.

"Liam?"

"We need to talk." He stood at the door. He couldn't go in. That would be pushing his limits.

She walked toward him, and all he could see were her shapely calves and long strides. Her skin glowed as if kissed by the sun. When she was standing not two feet in front of him, his gaze traveled up her body.

"You know, it's custom to look someone in the eye when you are trying to talk to them," she reminded him.

"I don't know what I'm doing here anymore," Liam confessed, meeting her gaze. "I was hoping you'd help me."

He took a step toward her and stopped a hair's breadth from touching her. "Elissa?"

"You had a reason when you came to my door. What was it?"

"Whatever it was, it can wait."

"Wait for?"

"This." Liam lowered his head to hers.

As though Elissa was standing outside of herself, as though in slow motion, she saw him coming toward her. A million thoughts ran through her head. Wasn't this what she wanted? For the last couple of days, everything had been leading to this kiss. If she were honest, she'd been playing that 'what-if' game. What if she and Liam had stayed together, if she hadn't been so scared of what others thought, and instead had trusted him?

All of those moments had led to Liam being in the same space, breathing the same air as her. Elissa should just throw caution to the wind and indulge. She could finally feel what it would be like to be in Liam's arms; to know what it would be like to be with someone she cared about. They were already married. Certainly, this was the right time. He was so close. His eyes were closed, and his lashes made half-moons on his cheeks. It would be perfect, if only she wasn't keeping things from him, and right now, she was trying to get him out of this marriage and at the same time, protect her aunt.

Elissa put her fingers to his lips. This was as close as she could get to him and still respect and protect what they might one day have. As hard as it would be, if she wanted to show she really cared about him, she had to push him away.

"Do you think if we kiss, I'll give some of the money back?"

Liam's eyes popped open. "What did you say?"

Elissa put her hands in her hair to hide the fact she'd slipped strands behind her ears.

"I'm just saying that eighty thousand dollars is a lot of money, and I know you are an expert negotiator."

Liam stepped back, his smile bitter. "There's a weird justice in you suggesting such a thing to me. The woman who asked for money is asking the man who gave it if he's trying to work some of it back. What irony!"

"I asked for the money as part of a deal we made. Don't make it seem like I'm the one who twisted your arm. You came looking for me, remember?"

"Yes, I came looking for you since you were applying for a job in my hotel. You didn't have to accept the check."

"According to the news, you needed someone to help you. The kind of help you were looking for doesn't come cheap."

"You can say what you want. I would have given you the job, it's about the money, Elissa. You could have walked away."

Elissa stepped back and turned away from Liam. She blinked away tears and continued doing her hair.

"Sue me. I'm human, and I did what I had to do."

"Why did you have to do it, Elissa?"

Elissa nearly broke under the whispered question. She wanted to tell him the truth but she couldn't. She'd never felt so conflicted. She knew she was protecting him the only way she could but she still felt like the worst person ever. Tears fell down her face. He was her one true love and she had to send him away.

"Listen, Liam. I owe you nothing. I've given you what you've asked for. Unless you want to renegotiate, I'd like you to step back and let me finish getting ready for my day."

"You know what? You're right. I'm going to stay in my lane. This is a business deal; nothing more."

CHAPTER TWENTY-ONE

Just when Liam thought he understood, Elissa turned again. Liam went to his office, grabbed his coat, and then went out the door. He couldn't see right or left. The only thing he knew was he needed to get out of the house and away from the woman he wanted and didn't want all at the same time.

When he went by Elissa's door, it was closed. For some reason, that just made him all the more frustrated. She wasn't even going to come out and talk to him about it.

Upon reaching the front porch, he realized he had no car and no way to get anywhere. Now he understood why so many people wound up at the church. It was probably the most centrally located place in town. He took a breath and got ready to set out. When he saw Colleen's car pull up, he kept his head down and hoped she would think he was being a pain and just ignore him.

"You can hunch your shoulders all you want. I guarantee people will still know who you are," Colleen called.

"Fine!" he snapped.

"Ouch! That was a bit abrupt. What happened? Did your stock go down today?"

"I'm not in the mood to talk."

Liam was already walking down the road when Colleen's car pulled up next to him.

"Listen, it seems like you need some space and someone who doesn't care about you, but can still make sure you get home ok. You want a ride?"

Liam looked over at Colleen in the car. This was his life now. The woman who probably hated him second to Elissa was the only one he could call a friend in this the town. He nodded, and she slowed so he could get in the vehicle. As soon as he sat down and buckled up, Colleen took off.

"Where are we going?"

"Somewhere we can drink the nectar of life and talk, because you surely look as though you could use someone to talk to."

Liam wasn't sure where that was, but right now, he wanted to stop talking. Maybe Colleen knew a bar they could go to. A suspicious pain spread through his chest, and he had a feeling it had to do with Elissa.

They wound up at the café he and Gran had been in before, when Gran had wanted to celebrate. The older waitress recognized him right away.

"Hey, you're back. How are you?"

"I've been better," Liam said.

The waitress waved him off. "You kids say that all the time. Life seems hard when you are in the middle of it. When you get to my age, you'll realize this was the best time of your lives." She took their order and came back with two cups of coffee, just like Colleen had ordered for them.

"Okay, tell me, what's the problem?" Colleen asked.

This is what he had come to. Colleen was his new confessor. Liam wished he could just call Travers and tell him to come back to Chusada, but Travers had to be in New York to take care of the board members.

Had he really told Travers that he needed to give Elissa time to do the party? Liam was twice the fool. She had made sure to hammer that point home today.

As Liam looked into his cup of black coffee, he wondered why he was sitting here and no alcohol was involved.

"Colleen, when you said we were going someplace, I thought you meant somewhere that served adult drinks," Liam said glumly.

"They do have adult drinks. Adults drink coffee, and that's what you're drinking. Besides, there are rumors this coffee is the best there is and simulates the feeling of euphoria." Colleen waggled her eyebrows.

"Euphoria?"

"Yes. The coffee is very expensive, as it's harvested straight from the dung of elephants."

Liam watched to see when she stopped jesting. Instead, she raised her cup and sniffed the rim. "I can practically smell India," she said before taking a sip.

Liam wasn't falling for it. He'd already been taken for $80,000. When the waitress passed by, he gave Colleen a smirk.

"Excuse me," he said to the older woman. "The coffee?"

The waitress perked up. "Do you like it? It's organic and straight from India. Excuse me; I'll be right back."

Colleen laughed and took another sip. "Don't knock it. Go ahead, try it out."

"Okay, I'll give it a shot." Liam took a sip, and then

Colleen put her cup down and sat back in the booth.

"So, what's the problem, Romeo?"

"I need to get home to New York City where things make sense to me."

"The only time you hear that from a man is when he's fighting with someone he cares about."

Liam shot Colleen a stern look. "Someone I care about?"

Colleen cocked her head to the side. "Yes, someone you care about. Are you thinking something else? If you are, let me help you get to the revelation. As much as it baffles me why anyone would want you and your troubles, you and Elissa really do care for each other."

Liam really looked at Colleen.

"You're Elissa's best friend?"

"Yes. I've been with her since before college and up until now. Why?"

"You would know why she asked me for the eighty thousand dollars."

Colleen stopped for a moment and then got the waitress's attention.

"Can I get some cheese fries?" Colleen asked. When the woman left, Liam waited.

"Colleen, help me out."

"I've already helped you out, rich man. I said you and Elissa care for each other, and that is why you are driving each other crazy."

"That's help?!" he asked incredulously.

"Yes, that is helpful! Do you think I like seeing Elissa unhappy? It's a good thing I saw a change in her attitude lately, because if I hadn't, I was thinking about bringing charges against you for making her miserable.

"You'd have to call your Rottweiler back to defend you. Lately, though, I've seen a change. It's one I haven't seen in Elissa for a while. As much as I hate to admit it, you are the reason for that change."

Liam heard the words, but felt conflicted and unhappy at the same time. He understood that Elissa cared, but he needed an explanation for the money. He was married to her, and most of the time being with her was like having a break from the world. She got him. Elissa talked to him about things going on in the world. She gave him a new world view, and she made him appreciate the simple things in life. All of those things she did, and still, she had asked him for the money. Was he just being taken for a ride by a woman who was better at deception than the rest?

"You don't understand, Colleen."

"You're a businessman, Liam. Sometimes you have to look for more than just what you see in front of you."

"True."

"Then start using some of that rich guy sense now."

Joy and another woman entered the restaurant and sat diagonally across. Colleen rolled her eyes, and Liam was at a loss why until he caught their conversation.

"Did you hear, Joy? Elissa's new husband was no more than her trying to get a job."

"What?" Joy's voice had a hint of fake surprise and outrage.

"Turns out she got married to get a catering contract for her failing business. It figures she would do that. You know, I remember something fishy being done at the church by the aunt, as well."

"What her aunt did was just a one-time thing," Joy said.

"A woman practically selling herself for a job? Well, that is a little over the top."

Joy dropped her napkin and reached over to pick it up. Her gaze shifted to the table he and Colleen were at.

"Oh, my goodness. It's Mr. Butler and Colleen. I hope you two are having a good evening."

"Oh, is that you, Joy?" Colleen said. "I didn't notice because we were sitting over here, minding our own business. That's what people do who have lives."

Joy resumed gossiping with the woman at the table.

Liam began to stand up so he could address the false rumor. Colleen placed her hand on his shoulder.

"Don't bother. It won't make a difference. Whatever you say, they will still come up with the same story. By the time they are done, they'll say you argued so much because it was true. When Elissa hears about this, she will be devastated."

"What? I don't understand. Elissa knows it's not true," Liam said.

"If Joy shared the gossip in front of us, it's because she's already told half of the town the same story. Sometimes what you know to be true isn't enough in a small town," Colleen said sadly.

Liam might not have all of the answers, but he had enough to take care of Elissa.

"We're good. Travers has already set up our travel, and we can actually leave Chusada tonight. She has a birthday party on Monday, but I'll send one of the other caterers from the hotel to take care of it. She can be angry with me later."

Colleen nodded as they got up from the booth. "I wouldn't worry about her being angry. It's my understanding that comes with marriage."

As Colleen drove them back to the house, Liam had to ask. "I'm going to have to ask you to come in with me."

"Of course. I told you, I'm her best friend since forever. Besides, I have to make sure you don't mess this up. Don't be discouraged, but I have to tell you, I'm not impressed with your skills so far in marriage."

Liam smiled. "Someone told me I'll get better with time."

"We can only hope."

Aunt Becky met them at the door. "I've already gotten a call about the gossip. Have you come to take care of my niece, your wife?"

Liam stopped at the door and looked at Colleen.

She brushed past him and walked in, muttering, "There's still the opportunity to mess things up."

Liam shook his head. "I've come to take care of my wife."

Aunt Becky smiled. "Then come in. I hope you have a plan."

"I'm already on it. Has Elissa heard the news yet?"

"No. She's been in her room. I was going to ask, it seemed like she is a bit upset." Aunt Becky gave Liam a stern look.

Colleen was already in his wife's room. When a small cry came from the room, he knew Colleen had told Elissa about the gossip.

Liam's hands clenched. He wasn't sure when it happened, but all of these people had become very important to him. When it mattered, they had all bonded together in order to make sure Elissa would be okay. That's what he imagined family would look like. This was his family now, and he would help set things right.

CHAPTER TWENTY-TWO

Butler Hotel, New York

Elissa's aunt had always said things would be better in the morning. Well, Elissa would have to tell her aunt it was true.

Now that Elissa had some time to really look at her situation, she realized she had been going about things the wrong way. All along, she had been surrounded by people who were there for her, who were her support system. Why hadn't she seen how much the people in her life loved her?

She lay in bed looking up at the vaulted ceiling and thinking the room would have been considered a mansion in Chusada. Elissa needed to get up at some point, but how could she face Liam? He'd been so caring and understanding last night, and she didn't want that to go away. While she replayed last night's events, she tried to fight off the wave of guilt of how she might have hurt him. She lazed about for a few more moments, and then something jumped on the bed.

Elissa's whole body tensed up until the object came into view: the prettiest white terrier she had ever seen.

Elissa sat up and the dog came into her arms.

"Hello, pretty. Who are you, and whose are you?" Elissa asked.

"His name is Mr. Butterscotch, and he's mine. You the gal that Liam done got hitched to?"

Elissa saw the elderly woman and had to hold the dog a little closer.

"Umm, yes, I am Mrs. Butler."

"Huh. I don't think you can be that, because I met Clara Butler. You gonna have to settle for 'the wife.'"

The older woman sat on the edge of the bed. Then she patted her side, and the dog wiggled out of Elissa's grasp and went to her.

"My name is Jane."

"And you are?" Elissa asked.

"I'm a lot of things." She smiled. "I'm the one Liam still owes a reward to, and between you and me, I make a little on the side watching him for Mrs. Butler."

Elissa was confused for a moment. "Oh, you mean for his gran?"

"Yup!" Jane's big smile showed off her missing front teeth.

"Do you live here?"

"Until I get what I think I'm due for payment. Besides, that boy needs some help." Jane stared at Elissa and then shrugged. "Maybe he doesn't need as much as he once did. Don't know. He's doing good so far, but you kids can be slow."

Elissa smiled. "Yes, sometimes we can be."

"Anyway, you need to get up. Liam has got some breakfast waiting for you out there, and Mr. Butterscotch can't run around if there is food. So you got to eat and then go. I hear you have a big day today anyway."

Elissa could feel her appetite coming back and she nodded.

"Will I see you later?"

"Of course. I live here, and if all I've been hearing is true, you will be living here, too."

Elissa got out of bed. The material of her two-piece night set glided across her skin. She picked up the robe on the chair and put it on, and when she opened the bedroom door to the living room she saw a breakfast set up for her and Liam. He was sitting in a chair on the side doing work. He'd waited, he hadn't started eating without her. He was dressed in gray slacks and a white shirt, the picture of professionalism. She'd seen this man taking care of his grandmother. Elissa had seen Liam care for those less fortunate. She had been falling in love with him all along. Her love for him was so clear. She just wondered if it was too late. Could they get through the obstacles before them?

Her legs were unsteady as she went toward him. When he smiled at her, she couldn't escape it. She loved him.

"Are you ready to eat yet? Mr. Butterscotch needs his daily run!"

Elissa looked over her shoulder and laughed. Liam laughed with her, and then she sat down to eat with her newfound love.

"I met your guest," Elissa said.

"'Guest' is such a loose term, but Jane lives here with her dog. She watches the place when I'm gone."

"She seems very—"

"Don't try to find the word, because there isn't one. I think we could look in the dictionary and see Jane in the place that word should be."

Elissa noticed how strong his hands were. How his jaw was perfectly chiseled and how he waited for her to finish every sentence and didn't interrupt when she was talking.

"Yes, I suppose so."

"Are you ready?" he asked, pointing to the tray.

Elissa nodded. He lifted the tops, and underneath were pancakes with blueberry smiles on them.

"I hope you like them. I asked Colleen what your favorite thing for breakfast was."

Elissa's throat clogged.

"Are you okay?" Liam asked.

"I'm just fine."

They ate in companionable silence. When she was done eating, she sat back and looked at Liam.

"Thank you for bringing me here." She studied her hands. How could she look into his eyes? Elissa knew how she felt, but wasn't sure where he stood.

"Elissa, look at me," Liam said gently.

She looked up.

"We both know there is more to it than that, those rumors are just that. They are petty lies put out by petty liars."

She couldn't keep his gaze and tried to hold back tears, but hot trails of moisture blazed down her cheeks. Liam's hand covered hers in her lap, and she had to hold back a fresh wave of tears.

"No more you and me. Now, it's gotta be us. Okay?" She heard the tray being moved aside, and Liam's hand in her lap guided her to stand. When she stood, she was pulled into his embrace.

"It may seem like we are the underdog, but we got this," Liam said.

"Hey, dogs are not under anything!" called out Jane. Elissa and Liam laughed, and then he tilted her chin up and placed a kiss upon her lips. While demanding, it didn't last long. The tenderness of the moment stuck with her.

"Don't cry, or I'll have to do something wild to live up to my reputation," Liam joked.

Elissa smiled. "Please. If you do, it will throw all of our work away. When do we see the board?"

"Well, I don't think we'll see the board, but one of their representatives will speak with us."

"When does that happen?"

"This afternoon."

"This afternoon! I need to find the right clothes."

Liam laughed. "Why is it when something happens, women need to find clothes? What comes out of your mouth is going to matter more than what you are wearing."

"I know you think that, but if I show up in jeans, it won't give the best impression."

Liam looked horrified for a moment. "I know I said what you wear doesn't matter, but I didn't think you'd consider jeans."

Elissa laughed. "Now who's concerned about clothes?"

CHAPTER TWENTY-THREE

Elissa and Liam had been called to the executive offices like children to the principal's office. She had asked Liam if he should go alone.

"No. It's us now remember? I don't do alone anymore. I'll be going forward with you by my side or not at all." He knew all the right things to say to her. Well, he'd said most all of them except the three words she needed to hear. But Elissa could wait for the elusive "I love you." To be fair, she hadn't said it, either.

When they got to the office, the woman at the front desk told them to go right in. Mr. Warner was inside with Chairman Carstairs.

Elissa didn't like the atmosphere at all. Everywhere she looked, there were signs that Chairman Carstairs was an old relic who liked other old ancient relics. She and Liam walked into the room, and Travers was sitting at a round table with a very round man: Chairman Carstairs. He looked like he should have a cowboy hat on and could be a sheriff.

Travers embraced her first. While he hugged her, he muttered in her ear, "Remember what you are here for and be quiet." Outrage was boiling her blood but she would wait to see what happened. When he pulled back, he said, "So glad you could come."

Then he turned to Liam and shook his hand. "Glad you could make it."

Chairman Carstairs stood up and held his hand out to Elissa.

"Hello, young lady. You are definitely the woman of the hour." He smiled. "It's my understanding that if it weren't for you, Liam here wouldn't be able to keep it together."

The chairman's hands felt cold and clammy. While he had a smile on his face, she heard the snake oil salesman in his voice.

"On the contrary," she said. "It's Liam who keeps us both on track. Isn't that right, Liam?"

Liam's mouth gaped for a moment. Then Travers kicked the back of his leg.

"She's too modest," Liam said lamely and heard the slight groan from behind him.

"Well, let's take a seat." The chairman gestured. "Liam, I'm glad married life agrees with you."

"Yes," Travers said. "It has greatly improved his demeanor and public works."

Carstairs smiled and looked again at Liam. "Yes, yes,

there is that. I don't want to waste our time. We all have things to do, and we all know why we are here. Besides, it's my understanding that new wives require lots of attention."

Liam smiled while Travers and Carstairs laughed. Elissa pasted on a smile and squeezed his hand. If Carstairs kept making those kinds of jokes, Liam wouldn't have a hand to use for anything anymore.

The chairman sat back in the low, black leather chair and clasped his hands together.

"Liam, the board has been so moved by your progress that we have reconsidered earlier thoughts of removing you. While we think you are doing better, we believe you will still need supervision. We, as the board, are willing to do that in the following way. You will retain the title of CEO, but all decisions will have to be cosigned by the board. We will retain fifty-one percent of the voting power. However, for all others concerned, you would still be the CEO of Butler Hotels. Those are our terms."

"I hear what you're saying, but I'm not sure about the execution," Liam said.

"The execution we can work on, but this is what we feel we can commit to," the chairman said.

"This isn't running a company. This is hobbling me, and if you don't agree with my decisions, then I'm stuck trying to undo your lack of vision."

The chairman sat up and got red around the collar.

"It may not be what you were expecting, but it is what we can do. It's the only option we will entertain."

Liam fought anger and hopelessness. "How about I have fifty-one percent for six months, and we see how that goes?"

"No. I'm afraid we are firm on this."

"Chairman," Travers said. "Can we have some time to consider how this will work?"

Carstairs stood and puffed up his chest.

"Look here. We have been more than patient. We can't give more time or space, as you may call it. This is a business, and—"

"Enough!" Elissa rose to her feet. "I thought we were here to have a discussion, but you are here to try to put Liam in his place. Well, I have news for you. He doesn't need to be put in his place, and you are going to need him way before he needs you. You want to know what you can do with that fifty-one percent, Chairman?"

"Listen, young lady. I'll admit you are easy on the eyes, but this is man's talk and—"

Liam stood up and put his arm around Elissa.

"I'm going to have to agree with my wife. You'll need me first. You know how it is with new marriages. The wife calls the shots, happy wife, happy life!" Hand in hand and heads held high, Liam and Elissa walked out the door with a shocked Travers and Mr. Carstairs staring after them.

Liam served ice cream to Elissa while they sat on the floor in the hotel room. Jane had taken Mr. Butterscotch out and said she needed to visit some of her friends. Liam wasn't really sure what that meant, but he wasn't going to dig too deeply. Earlier, he and Elissa had ordered in Chinese food. The action had brought the concerned chef knocking on his door and Liam had to calm the man down.

Sitting with his wife now, Liam couldn't imagine a better time. Liam wasn't one for secrets and his wife still had some. He smiled to himself. Some smart person had said he needed to understand things weren't always the way they seemed.

"Elissa?"

"Yes?"

"I have to ask you a question."

She smiled as she dug into her pistachio ice cream. "Go for it!"

"I can get the whole thing when we were in college. I was prideful and didn't like being called dumb."

"I would never call you dumb."

Liam held up his hands. "I never thought myself smart, so when I heard you would only be with a genius, I thought you were mocking me."

Elissa's eyes went wide, and then she covered her mouth. He could tell she was laughing.

"What's so funny?"

"It's beyond funny that I thought that then, and I believe now you are one of the smartest people I know."

Liam paused and gave her a long look. Elissa nodded, and he chuckled. "Well, I guess that's what happens when you know you have to fit into some pretty big shoes."

"I can see that," she said as she ate another mouthful.

"I will definitely take the compliment. The question I have is about the money."

"The road to perdition—"

"Elissa, you stood by me when I went to see the chairman. You stayed with me, and I may not have anything left now. I think we are at the point you can tell me about the money."

"Oh Liam, I've been so scared. I borrowed eighty thousand

dollars from Aunt Becky to start Green Magic, and it hasn't done well. That first day at the park when I went in to the church to look for Aunt Becky, I overheard her on the phone saying she was low on money and had to go back to work. So I needed the money from you so I could pay off the loan she took out when she gave me the money."

Liam smiled and put his ice cream to the side. "I hate to say it, but Colleen was right that things aren't always what they seem. Please don't tell her I said that because I will never live it down."

Liam leaned in and gently pressed his lips to Elissa's. Hers were cold and tasted like pistachio and sweetness. He didn't rush, and while before she'd just received the kiss, this time, she responded. A low moan came from her, and then he reached out and stroked her hair. As though his touch was electric, Elissa jumped back and put her hand over her mouth.

"Oh!"

"Yes?" Liam said, still leaning and waiting expectantly.

"There is more, I need you to sit back and listen to me," Elissa said. Liam could tell that whatever she was about to say must be important and had been weighing on her mind for quite some time.

"You're right. We should be completely honest with each other," confessed Elissa. "When you gave me the check, I immediately went to the investor to give it to him. I don't know if you remember Fred?"

"The odd guy who is kind of always alone?"

Elissa nodded. "I'm surprised you even remembered him."

"He was so smart, but never wanted to be in the group. He always wanted to leave it. We were just kids, and Fred had no looks, no money, and as far as the other guys were concerned, he had no say."

"Well, he grew up to be a miserable man who learned how to create retirement funds he could embezzle money from. He has been running some kind of scheme, and he has taken all of the money in the retirement fund that my Aunt Becky was in."

"Are you serious?"

Elissa nodded. Tears formed in her eyes. She had already put down her ice cream, and now she was wringing her hands in her lap.

"I'm still confused. What does this have to do with you?"

"When I went to give him the money, he wouldn't take it. He said if I put the cash in after everyone else's was gone, it would look like Aunt Becky had been in on taking the rest of the funds."

"You believe people will really think that?

Elissa sighed and then looked around the hotel room.

"What I do believe is that there are people like Joy in this world who will always think the worst of you. If it had just been me he threatened, it wouldn't have been a problem. But when I think about what this will do to my aunt, I can't think at all."

"Have you told Colleen?"

"No," Elissa whispered.

"First thing's first. In the morning, we will call our barracudas—"

"Our barracudas?" Elissa gave a tremulous smile.

"I'm sure we can find other names for them, but for right now, that will do. Between the two of them, they will be able to figure out how to deal with Fred. What is more important right now is that we agree not to keep secrets from one another."

"I understand what you are saying, Liam, but it is in my nature to want to protect those I love."

Taking her hand in his he said, "I'm not asking you not to. I'm asking you to let me help you protect her. Remember it's us now, we are in this together. She's my family now, too, is that too much to ask?"

Elissa moved closer to Liam.

"Can I ask you a favor?"

"Sure."

"Can you hold me for tonight?"

Liam thought about the kiss and how the heat of it had run through his body and fired him up to thinking how it would be to kiss her cheek and the place where she kept tucking that strand of hair. So when he gazed into her trusting eyes, he knew he'd give her anything.

"Of course," he said, "if you'll answer a question for me."

Elissa smiled and then nodded.

"Besides me being the smartest man you know, is there anything else you'd want to tell me?"

He wiggled his eyebrows to egg her on.

Her gaze went to the floor, as though she were plucking something up from the rug.

"I don't think so. I mean, I'll get around to telling you I love you when you tell me, but other than that—"

"Elissa Dane Butler, I love you. I love the you that goes out of her way to protect her family. I love the you that cares enough to fix ugly but tasty food. No matter what flavor you come in, I love you."

Elissa threw her arms around Liam. "When you say it that way, I love you, Liam Butler, my husband, my partner, but most of all, my friend."

I hope you enjoyed Liam and Elissa's story. If you'd like to know if Liam gets his spot back and what happens to Fred, you can read the next story with Travers and Colleen in *Love Saves book 2: It Shouldn't Be You.* To get you started I have included Chapter 1.

If you'd like to get more news from me sign up to my newsletter to receive updates on new releases, sale promotions, and free books.

susanwarnerauthor.com

It SHOULDN'T Be You

LOVE SAVES • BOOK TWO

SUSAN WARNER

CHAPTER ONE

Travers had been tracking Colleen all day. For a woman who had just gotten engaged to the biggest catch over three counties, she didn't look as thrilled as he thought she would be. Instead, she looked like a thief who was about to steal something. Just when he thought his imagination was pulling overtime, Colleen came out of the party and into the garden. He watched her reach into a bush and pull out a backpack. His curiosity was beyond piqued.

Following a short distance behind, he watched Colleen find a bush that was taller than her to offer some cover. She darted behind it and kicked off her heels then pulled a pair of sneakers out of the bag, along with a pair of jeans. She shimmied into the jeans, donned the sneakers, and took off her red dress, leaving her standing in her jeans and a matching red strapless bra. Travers would have bet money nothing could have fit under that dress, but he could see now he was wrong.

Just when he thought it couldn't get any weirder, she pulled out a brunette wig. Colleen pulled her hair into a bun so tight he winced. Then she planted the brunette wig on her head, making sure none of those lustrous red strands peeked out.

She stuffed her clothes in the denim backpack and then walked toward the valet section.

"Where are you going all dressed up, Red?" he muttered to himself.

Travers knew he should turn around and go back to the party. Colleen Bowers was the kind of woman a man would change his life for. She was smart, intelligent, and fearless. Not to mention tall. Colleen was the woman you hoped your daughters took after and the woman you wanted with you to go into battle.

The problem, of course, was that Travers was firmly married to his job, and a woman like Colleen wouldn't ever take second place. More importantly, a man who had a woman like Colleen wouldn't make her take second place. No, Travers's life was already planned out. He was the COO of Butler Hotels. His friend, the CEO, was having some issues fighting a takeover, but as soon as this issue was resolved, Travers was going to find a nice docile wife who liked to count his money, go shopping, and have a kid or two. Colleen didn't fit any of those characteristics.

Travers knew what he wanted, but he found himself continually drawn to the quick-witted shrew, Colleen. Five minutes ago, he thought this problem would resolve itself. As soon as she announced the date of the wedding today, Colleen was no longer available. Why was she messing up the plan?

Travers had stopped dating since he'd met Colleen. He wasn't a man to dine with one and think about another one. He had already scheduled two dates for next week since he knew Colleen would no longer be an option.

He watched her boldly walking up to the valet with a ticket in hand. Travers followed like a bear to honey. What was she up to? Why was Colleen destroying his week's schedule, and how did she think she was going to get her car in a brunette wig? What was so important that she needed to get dressed up in that outfit?

This made no sense. Colleen made him smile with her wit, and her unpredictable antics kept him intrigued. If he were honest, Travers would admit that he'd fantasized about what life would be like with Colleen. Every day would be new, exciting, and chaotic. For a man who scheduled everything, chaotic shouldn't appeal, but in Colleen's case, it was a draw he couldn't resist.

As he walked closer, he could hear the faint echoes of the conversation she was having with the valet.

"Ms., this is Ms. Bowers's car," the young valet said.

"I know whose car it is. I have a valet ticket. I'm doing an errand. Can you get the car?"

"I'm sorry, Ms., I'll need to see some I.D., or I'll have to call Mr. Chambers."

"I have a ticket!"

"I can put something in the car for you," the valet said hesitantly.

"I don't want to put something in it, I want to drive it!" Colleen protested.

She wanted to drive it. What was she doing? Travers looked over his shoulder and then back at Colleen, and the impossible came to him. Colleen was incognito escaping the engagement of the year!

Walking out of her engagement party hadn't been that big of a problem. They were all there to pat Luis Chambers, her fiancé, on the back. Colleen made it to her stash behind the bush, looking over her shoulder as she tried to escape casually. She took off her pumps and internally cried. Colleen was five foot eleven, but when she put on her power pumps, she was a comfortable six feet. She needed the extra height and confidence to walk boldly into rooms.

Now she was putting on her jeans, which weren't so bad, but these sneakers. The shoe guy had promised her they were comfy. After having her structured red-bottom heels on, the sneakers felt like she had mini airbags on her feet. She took off her silky dress and put on the rough shirt she'd bought. Life was about to get bumpy, so she better get used to it.

The coup de grace was the wig. Her bright red hair could be seen from anywhere. She had bought a beautiful, dull brunette wig and stuffed her tresses beneath it. She would stop every so often and wonder, *Do I need to do this?* Then she thought about Luis and his lawyer friends drinking at the bar last night. She had wanted to surprise him by showing up in this new wig so they could go places incognito. Instead, she had been surprised to find him in his cups with his friends. They spoke about how he would do his duty with me but would make sure he didn't tire himself out for the other women who wanted to be with an up-and-coming district attorney.

She couldn't believe how easy she'd been taken in. They had discussed it since Luis was coming to Chusada, that the district attorney spot was pretty much his, but she'd endorse him, and the town would agree. When she thought about how he had thanked her and told her she'd never regret it, Colleen felt like she should be putting on a dunce cap instead of a brunette wig.

Colleen knew what she needed was some time to think. She couldn't do that in town, and too many people would want to "help" her. All Colleen needed to do was get to her car. When she heard the football team was acting as valets, Colleen thought things couldn't be more in her favor.

She gave herself one final look, and a peek over her shoulder to make sure the coast was clear. She walked and talked with authority. The football captain was no match for her. She walked up to Greg Standers and presented her ticket.

Greg took the ticket and then gave her a once over.

"I'm sorry, Ms., this car belongs to Ms. Bowers."

"I'm well aware of who it belongs to. I have a ticket. I'm doing an errand. Can you get the car?"

Greg shrugged and looked really sorry but didn't seem as though he would budge.

"I'm sorry, Ms., I'll need to see some I.D., or I'll have to call Mr. Chambers."

"I have a ticket!"

"I can put something in the car for you," Greg said hesitantly. Colleen looked at Greg and then over her shoulder. They would notice she was gone any minute. It was impossible that she had planned for everything but hadn't thought about Greg, the head of the football team, becoming conscientious and not getting her car.

"I don't want to put something in it—I want to drive it," Colleen protested.

Greg held out his hands and gave his best smile. "I hear you, but Mr. Chambers paid us all a little extra to be extra careful about people getting in and out of this party. He didn't want anything to go wrong. I have to say, Ms., you don't look like you belong here. I'm willing to look over this if you go on your way. Otherwise, I'm going to have to call the police."

Colleen wanted to pull her wig off and eviscerate him with a tongue lashing that would make him cringe whenever he saw her. She was giving it serious thought when she heard a masculine voice clear his throat.

She started to nod her head and turned in the direction away from the voice when she heard the smooth tones of the one person she didn't want to meet, Travers Warner. She'd just keep walking. That was her intention until she felt his firm grasp on her shoulder.

"Peggy Lou, you beat me out here."

Peggy Lou! That was the best he could think of? She wasn't sure what his game was, but she'd play along. Beneath his tall-dark-and-handsome exterior hid a mindless troll, who would do whatever he had to for a dollar. It was just a distraction that he looked so good.

Colleen stood and then turned to Travers. "Hello, Travy."

Travers's smile widened. "Did you get the car?"

Greg interrupted. "Umm, I'm sorry, but she has the ticket for Ms. Bowers's car."

Travers gave his ticket to Greg. "I'll talk to Peggy here. Would you go get my car?"

Greg nodded and then ran off. Travers stood in front of

her with a smirk that might make a lesser woman melt at his feet, but not Colleen. She knew the beast that lived within. Travers Winters, COO, and best friend of her best friend's husband. It was only that fact that made him tolerable.

"I didn't know it was a thing to play dress-up at an engagement party."

"Well, you know it's never too early to insert a little intrigue into the marriage. Besides, I've been wondering what Luis really sees in me, and I thought I'd ask Luis to meet me somewhere. It's my suspicious nature as a lawyer and all."

Looking over his shoulder and back at her, he nodded. "Yeah, I can see how you would want some confirmation on this deal before it's signed and sealed. I think you're supposed to invite the fiancé to this escapade, though, aren't you?"

"I've got that all taken care of." Why was he staying? "I think your car will be coming up any moment. I don't want to hold you up." Certainly, that was the universal dismissal.

Travers reached into his jacket and pulled out his phone.

"Hey, why don't I help you out here? Why don't I give Luis a heads up so he can meet you now? That way, you don't have to go, and this concern will be put away."

Colleen thought she'd like to put him away. Then her phone rang. Out of instinct, she pulled it out, and the caller ID said, Luis. Nosy Travers looked right over her head.

"Oh, look, it seems like Luis is looking for his fiancée already. Go ahead and answer it. I'll wait."

Colleen rejected the call and then looked at Travers. It was all his fault. Whenever Travers was involved, her plans went south. He seemed so calm and collected, standing there in a dark suit and a pink shirt. What man could wear a pink shirt and still look so masculine? She knew the magic was in his eyes. They were sorcerer's eyes. They were brown at first glance, but on closer inspection, she always noticed the golden flecks in them that made him look like a wizard from old.

She wanted to say she wasn't affected by his general appearance, but the whole package only accentuated the brilliant mind housed within. From day one, she had mentally sparred with Travers, and he'd met her tit for tat. He made her feel petite because he was taller and had a body that was no stranger to the gym. When she was around Travers, she started to think there was merit to being a helper and helpmeet in a relationship, and that was when Colleen knew she had to keep him far away.

Colleen's mother had fallen for that trap. Her father had married her when she was a young law student, and she gave up her career to be a mother. Only to have her father cheat on her and leave her. Sure, her mother was remarried and happy, and her father was remarried and regretted the actions of his youth, but Colleen had been with her mother in the aftermath. Her strong mother had been reduced to tears and an abyss of loss. Colleen was not going that way.

"Well, it was nice seeing you, Travers, your car is here," she said with a big smile. Greg had just brought his car to the front and was holding out Travers's keys.

Then, before either of them could say anything, they both heard the faint calling of her name. It sounded like two men were calling for Colleen.

"Ahh, Peggy Lou, are you sure I can't give you a lift?"

Peggy Lou, the name grated on her. Thank goodness it wasn't her real name.

"I think I can make do; thank you, Travy."

Greg cleared his throat and looked at Colleen.

"Ms., I can't give you Ms. Bowers's car without her being here or Mr. Chambers."

Travers opened the door to his car. "I can drop you wherever you need to be, but the offer is a limited time only."

The sounds of her name got louder, and like a jackrabbit about to be pounced on by a wolf, she slid into the car.

"Get in and drive, Travy!"

Travers tapped the car door and gave her a smile. He pulled out a couple of bills for Greg and then got in the car.

"We need to leave now," she muttered under her breath.

"No worries, I know just the place to go," Travers said.

"Whatever, just move!"

Sweet Romances by Susan Warner

If you enjoyed this series, you could check out some of my other series:

Hidden Treasure series. Too often we forget what the real treasures are. Gold and money are temporary. A woman who loves and believes in you is priceless.

Inheritance Bay series. Inheritance Bay a place for second chances. It's where newcomers to the Bay find redemption, safe harbor and in some cases an inner strength they didn't know they had. What's for sure is unconditional love is an inheritance everyone deserves.

Love Happens series. Sweet small-town romances that show that love could be waiting for you right around the corner. Love is timeless and happens in all stages of life. Come and journey with the residents of Sweet Blooms as they discover true love can happen to anyone...unexpectedly. Welcome to Sweet Blooms, where love is always blossoming.

Love Endures series. Clean and Wholesome love doesn't just happen in small towns, they can happen in cities too. Second chance love stories that prove that love endures.

Silver Fox series. Love comes to us in all stages of life. Celebrate the couples that find life after kids have grown up and sometimes even after our first loves have passed.

Love Saves series. Sweet romantic comedy where couples find out what really matters in their lives, how opposites can do more than just attract and how love can save us all.

susanwarnerauthor.com

Ingram Content Group UK Ltd.
Milton Keynes UK
UKHW011833190323
418793UK00004B/596

9 781953 834492